THE HOLLOW REALMS

THE LIFE FEAST

JORDAN ALLEN

For my beloved family.

Contents

Prologue

It was a dark and drizzly night in the town of Bastia, much darker than usual as the storm clouds rolled in, covering up the radiant full moon that watched over the land of Roch. The streets below were quiet save for a few lone stragglers stumbling their way home after drinking a few too many ales in the last open taverns.

A cloaked man kept to the shadows as he walked hurriedly past the sleepy houses and tightly-locked shops. There were precious few lights glowing inside at this hour and that was all the better for him as it was imperative that he remained unseen.

"Woah there, laddie!" cried a dishevelled old man as the man in the cloak rounded a corner and collided with him. "You ought to watch where you're goin' or you'll be flat on the pavement. Not a threat or nothin', son, just an obser...observation."

The man in the cloak could smell the booze wafting off the old drunkard. "My sincerest apologies," he said, flicking a small silver coin at the vagabond who scrambled to catch his next drink. It was best to keep him happy and distracted, lest there be further unwanted attention drawn.

"Thank ye, friend," said the old man, examining the coin closely and grinning in glee. "Hmm, where'd he go?"

The cloaked man slipped away, striding through an alleyway as the faint drizzle picked up. By the time he had passed through the alley, that night's drizzle had turned into a downpour. Good; the louder the rain, the better. As he passed through the town square, all was quiet.

He wandered up to the fountain that continuously spouted water from the mouth of the majestic lion that topped it. A simple spell that kept the water eternally cycling, from dawn to dusk and then all over again, not hindered in the slightest by the storm. It was a curious little monument of Bastia, but the man had never paid it much heed.

He looked around uneasily, pulling his hood tighter around his head. What an awful place for a meeting when this town square was wide open. It would just take a crash of thunder and the wrong person opening their window to investigate to spot him standing there. Cloaked as he was, he feared that his face would be seen. He hoped the woman would hurry up.

As the minutes rolled by, he grew ever more impatient and had to fight to stop himself from looking around like a madman. Needing a distraction, he gazed into the water of the fountain and could see his reflection staring back at him, distorted by the raindrops and the splashes from the lion that sent ripples all across the surface.

"Am I making a mistake?" he whispered to himself, his mind feeling clearer by the minute. "This atrocity will not go unpunished, I know it will not. If not in this life, most certainly the next..."

"You would not be having second thoughts, my dear?" came a woman's sultry voice in his ear.

The man jumped a mile; he had not heard her approach for the rain beating against the cobblestones was almost deafening. He turned around and gazed upon her, but she too was cloaked in darkness except for the lower half of her alabaster face and luscious pink lips. He did not have to see her clearly to know that she was supremely beautiful. She was more beautiful than any woman he had ever seen; she was absolutely captivating.

"I...I don't want to do this," said the man shakily, averting his gaze. "They are innocents! They should not suffer so."

"They will live," said the woman, reaching up and caressing the man's face with her silken palm. "I only ask for the smallest piece of them so that I may remain as I am."

"I cannot do it," lamented the man. "I am sorry, I am so sorry..."

The woman turned the man's head towards her and planted a deep kiss upon his lips. He tried to pull away, but he gave in and returned the kiss. At first, it felt wrong, but then it felt as though his lips should never not be touching the woman's, so passionate was her kiss.

"You will do this for me, won't you?" asked the woman, pulling away.

"Yes," replied the man breathlessly. "Of course, my love. Anything for you. I would do anything to please you."

"Then go," she said as she took his hand and placed a small glass vial in his palm before folding his fingers around it. Even the gentle touch of her fingers upon his sent a wave of ecstasy through him.

The man nodded slowly and looked around the square once more before departing. He made his way to the north where the house he sought lay. He knew it well; oh, he knew it so well. It was here that he would most certainly be recognised should he be seen; it was here that the greatest point of failure lay. Yet, he would do anything to please his love, so devoted was he to her.

Arriving at the manor a short while later, he could see that the only light came from the servants' quarters. The guard that manned the front gate was passed out at the gatehouse with an empty tankard on the ground. He was snoring so loudly that the storm barely masked his flapping, nasal groans. Everything was exactly as he had orchestrated. The poor fellow would no doubt take a beating for this, but that didn't matter.

The man removed a key from within his cloak and opened the gate quietly, careful not to let the hinges creak too loudly; not that it would have been heard over the rain. He stepped inside, pushed it gently closed and then locked it behind himself. Should any ne'er-do-well pass by and fancy a chance at the lord's riches, they would not be getting through.

He looked around once more, taking extra care to make sure nobody was watching from the curtained windows. Once he was satisfied that he was but a phantom in these grounds, he walked hurriedly up the path, eager to get out of sight as quickly as possible.

All the man could think of as he walked around the left side of the house to the door by the kitchen was what the woman wanted. She was after something much more precious than riches and it would be the greatest gift he could hope to give to his love. It was something that could not be bought easily, at least not for very long. She was after beauty itself.

Chapter 1

Descent into Darkness

Caen walked along the road by the forest with a smile on his face. It was a pleasant walk after the storm of the previous night. The birds were singing their merry little songs right before the sun was due to rise and the dewy grass glistened as the moon faded away. Caen walked with a stride, his leather armour clean and his two swords pristine.

His dark cloak flowed in the light breeze and he tipped his wide-brimmed hat at the man on the road who was walking the opposite way. The man almost seemed to not notice him before the good-natured gesture. He froze in shock upon realising that he was not alone on the road this morning.

"Hail there!" called Caen, as though he had not a single care in the world. It was a stark contrast to the man who bore a look of panic.

"You must be mad!" called the man, scratching his arm nervously. He was middle-aged and evidently poor, but he didn't look too worse for the wear.

"Mad?" asked Caen, cocking his head to the side. "I am not mad, my friend, but I am in need of direction if you would be kind enough to help a stranger."

"Do not tell me you're seeking the—"

"Yes, indeed. I am seeking the Crypt of Raphael Montclair."

"I will not tell you the way, stranger," said the man, shaking his head emphatically. "Beg your pardon, but I cannot in good conscience send you to your death...or worse."

"You would not be sending me to my death. I will come back alive, I assure you."

The man looked at Caen with an expression of utter terror. "You're...you're one of them, aren't you?"

"Whatever do you mean?" asked Caen, feigning ignorance.

"You're a Hell Stalker."

"Was it the hat? The hat always seems to give it away. We don't all wear these hats, you know. I just think it suits me."

The man shook his head, looking nervously towards the hills in the east. "You're stark raving mad, you are," he said before pointing towards the west. "If you truly have a death wish, that's the way you ought to go. Over the hill and through the trees. But don't say I didn't warn you."

"Excellent," said Caen, giving the man a courteous nod. "Much obliged, Mr...what was your name?"

"Fortesque," he replied. "Vincent Fortesque."

Caen gave him a satisfied smile and, quick as lightning, drew one of his blades and cut Fortesque's head from his body in a flash. The man's body turned to a pillar of ash and then crumbled, blowing away in the wind, leaving no trace behind.

"I thought so," muttered Caen. "It's a good thing I was right too or I would have quite the mess on my hands. Perhaps if I hadn't met your former family in town, I may have fallen for your innocent ruse. In any case, rest in peace. May your sundered soul find its way to the True One."

The Hell Stalker chose to take the vampire at his word and headed west towards the hill, away from the rising sun of the east. He walked along as the sky grew ever brighter in the early hours of the day. Daylight, of course, was what he wanted, for it was one of the few things that the vampires truly feared. They would not dare rear their ugly heads in sunlight; they would burrow themselves in the dark crevices of the Outer World until night fell once again.

Caen was a man who was used to the road, but it was not used to him. Everywhere he went, he sought trouble, for that was in his nature. He chose the life of a Hell Stalker—a hunter of the demonic and unnatural—thinking that he could make good use of his combat prowess and earn some coin along the way, but the coin never seemed to last very long.

When people saw him coming into town with his dark attire, pointed nose and wavy brown hair, they would always point and speak aloud. "He's going to bring trouble with him," while giving him a wide berth.

To them, he was unclean and they could not comprehend that every life he took was in service to the world, not with a desire to bring chaos and disorder. No, those were the forces that he fought against. It just so happened that when fighting these forces, you uncover the darkness that was there all along. People, of course, do not like the truth despite what they may claim.

"The Outer Sentinels do not receive such harsh treatment," he would grumble regularly to those who would listen. "Their divine magic and affiliation with the church might have something to do with it. If I strolled into town in shining plate and preached the True One's word about town, I would no doubt receive a much warmer reception."

Crossing over the hills and walking amongst the trees, Caen could see a few sets of tracks, some human and some animal. He examined the footprints closely, gleaning what he could from them. One of the sets of tracks was likely from a man who had been gathering firewood as his muddy steps led up to a felled tree that was missing more than a few chunks from it. Another led towards a small flowing river, yet they would certainly not be the tracks of a vampire as they could not cross the running water.

Caen leaned against a tree and started to think. There would surely be an easier way of finding the crypt rather than poking his head between every bush along the way. He would be here until nightfall if he was to do that and he would rather get to work in the daylight so the vampires could not follow him to the surface should he need to flee. He sighed a heavy sigh as he leaned back and looked up to the leaves of the trees.

"Well now," he muttered to himself as he caught sight of something both welcome and unwelcome, "what do we have here?"

On the branches of the particularly thick tree he was leaning against were a few lurkers with their black-as-night wings wrapped around their bodies. The bats hung upside down and watched him intently, not in the least bit frightened of him—though they ought to be. The vampires knew he was here already, or at least they would very shortly. Their messengers would surely tell them the first chance they got.

Caen chuckled to himself and picked up a large stone from the woodland floor. He threw it at the bats who scattered widely and flew frantically away into the deeper reaches of the forest, all eventually converging together in a large swarm. The Hell Stalker gave chase, intent on keeping his eyes on his dark, shadowy guides.

"There you are," whispered Caen as the bats flew towards a small stone building and into the dark archway that sat in the centre, welcoming whatever prey would dare venture inside. "Montclair, Montclair, are you home?" asked Caen quietly, drawing his two swords and gripping them so tightly his knuckles grew whiter than ever.

This was the part he loved the most; the kill. With any luck, Montclair would be doing what vampires do. He would be lying in his coffin or sarcophagus, whichever he had chosen to be buried in, and his neck would be exposed. A clean cut, his body would be ash and Caen would be back in town by noon to collect his silver.

He stepped onto the moss-covered stone staircase leading downwards. There were flames flickering in small lanterns down below already indicating that the bats had indeed warned their master. Whether he went back to sleep or not, Caen did not care. He moved carefully with the glistening moss still slick from the rainfall of the night before.

He froze. He could have sworn he had heard the sound of something scraping against the stone at the base of the stairs. Something was waiting around the corner for him, he was sure of it. He moved to the bottom of the staircase, his footsteps quieter than a whisper, and pulled out a single silver piece from a pouch on his belt. He tossed it straight ahead and the second the coin flew past the corner, something immediately lunged for it, thinking it was the Hell Stalker himself.

Caen thrust a sword forward, skewering the bald, sallow-skinned and red-eyed vampire through the chest. It turned to look at him with its smiling fanged face, but that excited look of hunger suddenly morphed to fear as Caen's second blade wedged itself thoroughly in the vampire's neck. The Hell Stalker kicked the vampire back, pulling out his first sword and took two more swift swings at the wretched undead, cutting the head from its body before it crumbled into ash just as Fortesque had done.

Looking up the hall, Caen could see that all was quiet. Montclair probably didn't think much of him if he had only sent one of his minions to attempt an ambush. With that sloppy three-hack job to the vampire's neck, he joked to himself that perhaps Montclair was right. He blamed his poor form on the lack of range of motion in the tight tunnels of the crypt but vowed that the next vampire would be dead in two swings or less. Even with nobody to see, he had a high standard to maintain.

Caen crept quietly down the crypt, holding his swords close to his body. If the breathless vampire could give away its position, he could too. Vigilance was paramount. The crypt was littered with cobweb-covered skulls on small ledges, while protrusions of stones from the arches and pillars that lined the walls jutted out at strange angles. The ceilings were surprisingly tall, supported by arches standing strong against the weight of the soil above, yet every so often a tree root had forced its way through the bricks and started slithering down the walls.

Suddenly, a pair of vampires leapt from the shadows at Caen with their sharp daggers raised high. He parried the strikes with sweeping swishes from his swords, clanging steel against steel. The vampires were ferocious in their attacks, swinging with both their daggers and sharp claws wildly. Caen met each swift strike with a well-placed block of his own, but he was on the defensive; he would have to split their focus to defeat them.

"Farewell," he said to the fanged pair, turning tail and running back the way they came.

Stunned for a moment at his abject cowardice, the vampires then pursued him down the stone tunnel. As soon as one rounded a bend, a sword swung around the corner pillar like a guillotine, beheading it and turning it to ash.

The second vampire recoiled as Caen leapt out and kicked it square in the chest. It fell backwards and the Hell Stalker leapt upon it with his sword raised high and skewered the wicked undead through the neck with his two blades. He pulled them apart, ripping the vampire's flesh and severing its head. Seconds later, he was dusting the ash from his boots before making his way deeper into the crypt once more.

"I should have brought a magical light," said Caen as the flickering flames vanished leaving only darkness ahead. His friend, Lestrange, had often told him that he should learn a few token spells to help himself with his slaying endeavours, but Caen insisted that he did not have the time and the next job awaited him.

"You don't need to learn how to cast them *well*," Lestrange would say.

"Well, I'm not going to learn to cast them at all," Caen would retort, prompting a shake of the head and a sigh.

"A spell to heal an injury, a spell to light the way, and a spell to open locks. Simple little spells that would make your life much easier."

"I would rather not," he would say as Lestrange let out a sigh of exasperation.

As Caen pressed on, the faint outline of a wooden door grew visible through the shadows. There was light coming from behind it. Surely the crypt couldn't be much bigger. Montclair was a mere baron in his old life and would not have been blessed with the sort of crypt a mourner would get lost in, but perhaps the rank of a baron had meant more two centuries ago when he was still breathing air and had rightful claim to the forest above.

Caen clutched his swords and pushed the door open with his foot. The light from many lanterns brought the room to full illumination and he could see the undead baron himself, Raphael Montclair. He had slick black hair that swept over his ears and onto his shoulders along with a sharper nose and chin than even Caen himself had. He wore a dark jacket and a clean ruffled shirt underneath with a silver amulet around his neck. He held a cup in one hand, drinking deep on a fine red wine. It would not have been an unusual sight in Roch to wander into a noble's house and have seen this, but on the table before him sat what unsettled Caen more than anything he had seen in weeks.

It was a young woman, no older than eighteen years old lying naked and motionless on the table. Her body was deathly pale, far beyond her natural fair complexion. She was on the verge of death with multiple bite marks across her neck, chest and stomach. Montclair stared at Caen with a look of satisfaction on his face as he licked blood from his fangs and took a sip of his wine.

"I know why you're here, Hell Stalker," said Montclair, his voice cold and deep. "You're too late to save the girl, she's got precious little blood left in her. Just enough that I can have some dessert before I sleep for the day. But what a feast the delightful Genevieve was, might I say. Delectable beyond your wildest dreams. A pure virgin treat in every sense of the word."

"Tragic as it may seem," replied Caen, his eyes focused on the vampire and watching for any sudden moves, "I am not here for her. I am here for you alone, Montclair."

Montclair laughed loudly. "The poor damsel does not even have enough love from her family to merit a rescuer?" Montclair put his cup on the table and leaned forward. "Tell me then, dark hunter, whose family sent you to kill me? It must have been someone I was recently acquainted with."

"It was the Dubois family."

"Dubois...Dubois...hmm," muttered Montclair, pretending to think for a moment. "Ah yes!" he exclaimed. "That lovely young redhead. I made her one of my own, in fact. A precious little thing, she was, but she did not take to our ways all too well. She was slain within a week of being sired. *That* was the true tragedy of Helen Dubois."

"You know what comes next, Montclair. I presume you will not go to the ashen grave quietly?"

"Of course not," scoffed Montclair. "I shall not go at all."

"Suit yourself," said Caen with a small shrug of his shoulders.

Montclair picked up his cup of wine and threw the rest into his mouth before slamming the cup on the table. He leapt from his seat, over the girl and onto the table. Before his boots even touched the polished oak, his appearance shifted. His ears grew pointed, his nose turned up like a snout and the whites of his eyes faded to jet black. His pale skin was now a sickly grey as his flesh bloated and stretched with thick ridges rising from his brows and running across the top of his head. The carefully maintained image of the dignified nobleman now replaced with a horrific monster; a vampire lord who had assumed his true, grotesque form.

Caen braced himself as Montclair jumped from the table and glided towards him with incredible speed. The vampire lord struck at him with his sharp claws, but Caen would not allow a finger to be placed upon him. A claw was swept aside with one blade while another cut into the vampire's arm. When Montclair lunged at him, Caen deftly moved out of the way and kicked the vampire forcefully in the leg. Caen knew that when he had to deal with multiple foes, he would struggle, but with one foe—even one as powerful as this—he flowed like water.

Montclair screeched and yelled in frustration as the Hell Stalker blocked and parried each attack, almost as though he was toying with the greater undead. To be insulted in such a mocking way by a mere mortal was an affront to his vampiric nature and to his blood-fuelled power.

Not content with such appalling treatment, the vampire lord's strikes became more forceful and rapid. He would use his full power to overcome this invader in his home and Caen would fall to him. As a Hell Stalker, the man could not be turned, but he could certainly be made to suffer for a very long time.

Caen continued to block and parry, cutting the vampire where he could, but no sooner did Montclair bleed than each wound was mended. He had just fed and he was at the peak of his strength. Caen knew he would not stand a chance at winning this fight by merely trying to overpower his foe, he had to play it smarter than that. Something he was keenly aware of before even setting foot in the vampire's crypt.

"Die, you worm," spat Montclair as he reached for Caen's throat, only to be brushed aside once more.

The vampire's fury was reaching its peak and his mind grew more and more feral as he was continually outwitted by the smirking Hell Stalker. This called for desperate measures before he lost himself to rage, but his next move was nothing he couldn't recover from.

Montclair grabbed hold of Caen's twin blades, the sharp edges cutting into his mutated hands. Saliva dripped from the vampire's mouth as he smiled and wrenched the blades from the human. He tossed them across the room, leaving Caen without weapons and at the non-existent mercy of his undead foe.

Smiling wide in his certain victory, the vampire lord lunged once more and grabbed Caen by the neck, pulling him in to bite. Suddenly, Montclair screeched so loudly that the flames in the lanterns shook and he recoiled in pain as his hands burned. He released Caen, staring at his hands in horror as they steamed and bore raw flesh that did not heal as it should have.

Caen flashed a devious smile at Montclair. "Do you think I am foolish enough to not visit a holy man for a blessing against your evil?" asked the Hell Stalker, waiting for the vampire to take his next piece of bait.

Montclair leapt across the room and grabbed the handle of one of Caen's blades, only to drop it in pain too. He turned around to find another weapon, only to see Caen jumping at him with a wooden stake in his hand. The Hell Stalker plunged it deep into the vampire lord's chest, where his once-beating heart lay. The evil baron's contorted face was filled with unmistakable fear as he turned to ash and crumbled away, his time finally up.

"Good riddance, Montclair," said Caen, looking at the pile of ash that had caused so much trouble to so many people.

He retrieved the amulet that lay within the pile and walked over to the girl on the table. She was in an unmoving daze but there was a pleading in her eyes. A pleading that was asking him to make the pain stop and to stay with her so that she was not alone when she slipped away.

"I am sorry this happened to you," said Caen, kneeling by her side. "I assure you that Montclair will never trouble anyone again. He is dead and he will not be coming back."

Caen held the girl's hand as he spoke aloud a prayer to the True One. He asked the almighty deity to guide this young woman's soul to the Inner World, where she may be at peace, free of this mortal coil that had brought her only suffering. He prayed for the end of the evil that the dead baron had inflicted upon the world and that his sired vampires would meet their end in sunlight before the day was done.

The Hell Stalker stood up and could see that the girl had died while he was praying. It was a sign, he knew it. The True One had answered the first part of the prayer and drawn her soul away from the darkness. Caen had faith in the almighty divine that the second part would be answered too.

"What was your name?" Caen asked the dead girl. "I was never too good at remembering names. Did Montclair call you Genevieve? I suppose that does not matter now. Be at peace, my dear."

He retrieved his swords from the floor and walked from the room. He would scour the rest of this crypt in case any further creatures of the night were lurking in the shadows. He was feeling bright and optimistic even in the darkness of the underground. The journey to collect his prize was only a mere two hours on foot. Once that was out of the way, he would indulge at the local bar before making his way home to Bastia.

Chapter 2

The Lord's Request

The midday sun of Bastia lit the bustling Rochian town intermittently as the clouds rolled by. A storm was fast approaching and everyone was hurrying to wrap up their business before the rain started to fall. The only man in town who had not a care in the world was lying on the low wall around the edge of the fountain in the town square with one leg folded over the other and his wide-brimmed hat covering his face as he rested.

Caen was wide awake underneath the hat, but he was enjoying his relaxation time. The sound of the endlessly flowing fountain was as soothing to him as knowing that he had no place to be while everyone else was frantically scurrying. Every now and then he would laugh to himself as he thought about this.

He had arrived home three days ago and he had yet to hear of any news about any demon or monster attacks. All was quiet for him, but he had plenty of coin to see him through the next few weeks until work turned up on Lestrange's doorstep. He would no doubt hear about something soon enough.

"Master Caen?" came a clear and posh voice from above him as though responding to the thoughts drifting through his mind.

Caen lifted his hat up and saw the silhouette of a man, his face obscured as the sun shone behind him, enjoying a brief respite from its time behind the clouds. "That's me," said Caen, putting his hat back over his face.

"Your presence is requested at Lord Legot's manor at once," said the man, maintaining his politeness despite Caen's indignation.

The clouds rolled over the sun once more and Caen lifted his hat once again. He could see that the man speaking to him was a young fellow in a blue tunic lined with gold trim woven into a series of loops. He wore a matching hat with a plume of small white feathers sticking out to the left side. The expression on his haughty face was not one of amusement as he watched Caen lazily lying at the edge of the fountain; he was a man on a mission and clearly saw Caen as a layabout.

"At once?" asked Caen.

"At once," repeated the envoy, sternly.

"It must be something very important if I'm required at once, sir. Might I trouble you for an explanation as to why I'm so urgently requested before we set off?"

"You may not," said the envoy. "It is a highly private matter that the lord would discuss with you in person."

"I see. And he's too busy to come down here himself, is he?"

The envoy ignored the snarky comment, sensing that he was being baited into a response. "I have been told to tell you that the reward will be worth your time."

"Oh? Well, in that case, I will not keep him waiting any longer," said Caen, swinging himself up and onto his feet. He stood at least a foot taller than the envoy who wasn't much past five feet tall. "Lead the way," he said, removing his hat and gesturing towards the north where he already knew the lord's manor lay.

Everyone in Bastia knew of Lord Legot and the grounds that he called home, even if they had never seen anything of it except for through the barred gate. Those who did have the privilege of being allowed inside would tell tales of the tall trees and vibrant flowers that were planted all throughout the most beautiful place in the town.

The envoy gave a curt nod before walking briskly northwards. Caen placed his hat back on top of his head and strolled along after him, his longer legs making it easy to catch up to the small man with little effort on his part. It helped that the town square was much quieter than it had been even a few minutes ago and there were precious few people to get in the way.

As they walked, the clouds overhead grew darker and a light drizzle started. Caen held out a hand and felt the rain on his palm. He hoped this was not an omen of bad things to come. He then remembered that in his line of work, there was rarely a good omen. He let out a small chuckle to himself about this. The Hell Stalker would often attract funny looks because of how he made himself laugh.

Bastia was a lovely little hive of activity in the heart of Roch, even if the cobbled streets were now quiet. Anything you could hope for could be found here. Need a new tunic? Reginald's Silks was there for the rich and Pierre's Garbs and Garments was there for the poor. Weapons? Caen's friend Lestrange would no doubt have something that would suit any man, from bounty hunter to soldier. Beautiful women? Well, there was a reason foreigners flocked to Bastia and brandished their gold and silver in the hopes of bringing home a wife. Even throughout Roch, Bastia was renowned for its women, so much so that there were rumours abound of the water sources being infused with some sort of potion.

"What's your name?" Caen asked the envoy after a couple of minutes of walking along the main street.

"Hugo," replied the envoy bluntly, clearly not looking for a conversation. The man was focused on doing his job quickly and well with no desire to exchange as much as a pleasantry. Caen admired his dedication, even if he knew they would not get along too well.

The mismatched pair walked in silence until they reached the gate to the lord's manor. Hugo cleared his throat when they arrived and a young fellow who was guarding the gate from a small hut with a wide-open window hole stood up in a hurry. He scrambled over to the gate and opened it for the two men, who proceeded to walk up the paved path.

The lord's garden was immaculate with tamed green grass and groups of trees gathered in neat clumps throughout the walled estate. As the stories had promised, there were flowers planted of every colour of the rainbow tastefully grouped into complimenting bunches and spread across the land. In the quieter reaches of the grounds, Caen could see stone statues devoid of any dirt or moss that depicted everything from dogs to birds to Outer World goddesses.

The manor ahead was anything but symmetrical with windows of inconsistent shapes across the three or four levels of the aged building. The right side of the manor jutted out much more prominently than the left and told Caen that there must have been a wonderful dining room there that every noble in the land would dream of being invited to. Atop the roof of the outcropping that housed the front door was the flag of Roch—a pale green flag with a yellow lion facing to the right.

Caen glanced to the left and could see a man hauling a cart around the corner; it was filled mostly with rich green vegetables and a few fruits of red, orange and yellow; some were local and some were not. He must have been heading to the kitchen to restock for dinner this evening. The lord would eat well tonight, there was no doubt. Caen was sure that was the case every day.

Hugo pushed open the front door and led Caen inside the large main hall. The chessboard-patterned floor was lit by the daylight pouring in through the large windows across the front wall. The light bounced off the suits of armour and glazed blue vases adorning the edge of the room. Everything in sight was neat and clean, exactly as it should be and without a single speck of dust out of place.

Staring at him from atop the grand staircase was a large portrait of the lord and his children. The lord himself was a tall man whose auburn hair had receded into a widow's peak and his sharp nose could have put a man's eye out. His son was his double but with fewer wrinkles and a much lower hairline. His daughters were a set of twin girls, both of whom were young and beautiful with faces full of freckles masked by the powdered pale makeup they wore. Caen had heard that the lord was widowed in a tragic accident a decade ago, leaving him to raise his three children alone with the help of two dozen servants.

"This way," said Hugo as Caen stopped and stared at the portrait.

The envoy led Caen up the stairs and he saw the same young man from the portrait leaning against the bannister on the walkway above. He watched intently as the Hell Stalker climbed the stairs, but he did not say a single word. This was Guillaume Legot and he was well known around town for his womanising ways, but he would never fraternise with the lowborn publicly. He would certainly never be seen with the likes of Caen, someone with as filthy a job as hunting monsters.

Caen and Hugo reached the top of the stairs and the envoy led Caen around to the right and down a darker corridor lined with faintly glowing lanterns. There were no flames within the lanterns, instead, they each contained a single orange crystal. Caen had not seen glowing stones such as these before, but they were no doubt expensive and hard to come by. He would remember these should he ever feel like splashing out on a better light source than fire. He of course knew what Lestrange would say to him.

"If you could use magic, you would not *need* to keep spending money on torches!"

Hugo stopped outside a thick oak door and held up his hand to signal for Caen to wait. He used his other hand to rap on the door with his knuckles.

"Yes?" came a voice from the other side.

"Lord Legot," said Hugo loudly. "I have brought the man you requested, Caen the Hell Stalker."

"Send him in," said Legot. "You are dismissed, Hugo. Thank you."

"Yes, my lord."

Hugo opened the door, allowing Caen into the room, and then closed the door behind him. Lord Legot was sat at a large desk with a stack of papers just to his side and a single sheet directly in front of him. He set the swan feather quill he was holding down and moved the papers out of his way, gesturing for Caen to stand before his desk.

"Welcome, Caen," he said pleasantly, but it was a forced pleasantness. His voice was raspy and strained as though he wanted to get the point of the summoning quickly. "Do you have a family name or a title?"

"I do," said Caen.

It was clear that the lord had wanted a proper answer. "Well?" he said when Caen chose not to elaborate.

"I keep it close to my chest," replied the Hell Stalker. "The less others know about me, the better. I'm sure you understand."

"I would not have a week ago," said Legot solemnly before sighing. "Now I do indeed understand. I shall simply refer to you as Caen if that will do. It is not intended disrespectfully so please do not take it as such."

"It won't be taken disrespectfully," said Caen somewhat dismissively. "What can I do for you, Lord Legot?"

"I shall get into it then," said the lord grimly, but looking somewhat relieved. "Four nights ago, my daughters, Amélie and Celine, were kidnapped while they slept. Two girls, sixteen years of age...and they just suddenly disappear. The town guards have tried to find them, but their investigation yielded nothing. I would like for you to try and find them."

"I'm not simply a mercenary for hire," said Caen. "I only take on jobs where there's the known involvement of undesirables. Demons, undead, monsters. Creatures you would certainly not want crossing your path."

"I am aware of what being a Hell Stalker entails," said Lord Legot, but Caen held back a laugh at this comment. "I believe there is indeed a monstrosity involved in this abduction."

"In that case, I'm all ears, Lord Legot. Tell me what you know."

"I brought in a specialist to take a look at their rooms where they were last seen. He found small clumps of hair on the floor, caught between the floorboards. He is certain that the hair comes from a lycanthrope...a werewolf."

It was a full moon four nights ago. Caen remembered it clearly.

Legot continued. "I spoke to a priest at the

temple and he said that their men, the Outer Sentinels, were stretched too thin to act immediately. It would be two weeks before they would be able to search for my daughters. I fear that by then it will be too late. It may already be, but still, I must know what happened to them."

"What's the payment?" asked Caen.

"Three hundred silvers to bring them home or recover their bodies along with the knowledge of what happened to them."

"That's per daughter, yes?"

Lord Legot closed his eyes and breathed deeply, trying to mask his anger at this perceived extortion. "Yes," he said in a hushed voice, "per daughter."

"Should the worst come to worst and I am only able to find a mutilated corpse, how can I confirm it is one of them? I pray this is not the case, of course."

"With any luck, they will be wearing their rings still. They never take them off and they are nowhere to be found in the house. They're simple silver bands with identical emeralds encrusted around them."

"Has anybody come forward seeking a ransom?"

"No," said Legot. "That is what confuses me most. I had expected it by now, yet still, there is nothing. If it is not about money, I do not understand what it could be about. Perhaps someone seeks to hurt me by taking away two of the things in the Outer World that are most precious to me."

"You've questioned your men?" asked Caen. "Your servants?"

"Thoroughly," said Legot firmly. "If anyone here had any involvement then they are excellent liars. The guard on duty was drunk and asleep the night it happened and he has been removed from his post. He was not a willing participant in their abduction, that much is clear to me, but I saw to it that he was punished for his negligence regardless."

"And your son?"

"My son?" asked Lord Legot, affronted. "The lad has never put a toe out of line in his life. If you are insinuating that he wants all of my money when I die, I suggest you take it back as he knows that he will be well taken care of when that time comes. Do not dare bother him with such a matter, the poor boy has enough to deal with right now."

"The question had to be asked," said Caen, turning towards the door. "If there is anything else I need, I will be back."

"You can see yourself into the manor, should the need arise. I will let the servants know that you are to be allowed the freedom to come and go as you please."

Caen looked over his shoulder. "That would be most appreciated, Lord Legot."

"And Caen."

"Yes?" said the Hell Stalker as he reached for the door.

"It is not public knowledge that my dear daughters are missing. Please keep it that way for the time being. If the werewolf is a resident of Bastia, the last thing I want is for the kidnapper to be the talk of the town, to hear his deeds mentioned, and get spooked. He may start acting irrationally or flee beyond our reach."

"I won't say a word, I promise you that, Lord Legot."

And with that, Caen departed from the room. He walked back towards the stairs only to find the lord's son waiting for him by the bannister. He beckoned Caen over, not seeming to care that he was going in that direction anyway. He had a haughty air about him, very much like Hugo, which Caen did not like in the least.

"Hell Stalker, a word," he said.

"Yes, Master Guillaume?" asked Caen in a mockingly respectful tone that was lost on his target.

"You are aware of my name?"

"There are few in town who are not, especially the women."

Guillaume cleared his throat. "Well now," he said awkwardly. "That is neither here nor there, is it? We have more important matters to discuss. I presume that you have agreed to my father's request?"

"I will be taking the job, yes."

"It is imperative that you find Amélie and Celine alive. Do you understand me?"

Caen nodded slowly. "If they are still alive, I will bring them back that way. I can't promise you anything more than that."

"Yes, naturally," said Guillaume, then looking from side to side to make sure that none of the servants were lingering within earshot. "I have been quietly conducting an investigation of my own. It is not that I do not trust my father and his methods, I simply believe my perspective and connections may yield a more effective way of getting some answers."

"And what have you found?" asked Caen, seeing where this was going.

"There is an old fort on a path through the forest, just off the western road out of Bastia. It is inhabited by a group of werewolf bandits who think it good sport to attack merchants and stragglers as they make their way out of town. I would bet my entire inheritance on their involvement in some way."

"I am familiar with the road. There is a guard outpost not too far out from the town limits, is there not?"

"Of course, there is," said Guillaume. "But the fort is further past that. What better place to strike could there be? The travellers pass by the outpost and are days away from the next town or village so nobody will know they are missing for almost a week after they vanish."

"And you think these werewolves are the ones who have kidnapped your sisters?"

"I suspect so, but could not be certain. It lines up with what was found in their rooms. It is the best explanation there is for the time being."

"That is very interesting and I will look into it," said Caen. "You'll forgive me, but I must ask. Is there anything else you've found?"

"No," said Guillaume, nodding towards the stairs. "You are free to go, Hell Stalker. I wish you the best of luck."

Caen departed with a swoosh of his cloak, walking down the stairs and out the door of the elegant manor. He couldn't explain why, but he was very much glad to be on his way. He was far from a self-conscious man, but being in the manor did not suit him. He would far rather be digging deep in the bowels of the Outer World for something to kill.

As he strolled down the path with the pouring rain beating down on him, his first thought was to head into town and check with Lestrange to see if he could verify Guillaume's claim about the werewolves; the man was a fountain of knowledge. If there was a grain of truth to it then he would arm himself to the teeth and take out those overgrown hairballs.

Chapter 3

Sharp Claws

"You're going werewolf hunting?" asked Lestrange with a raised eyebrow while pushing his spectacles back up his nose. "What sort of job have you gotten yourself this time?"

"One that involves werewolves," said Caen.

"I gathered that," said Lestrange with a frown.

"Keep it hush, but it's the lord's daughters."

"They're werewolves?"

"No, they're missing?"

"Taken by werewolves?"

"Seemingly," said Caen, nodding his head. "Now, what have you heard about werewolf attacks along the western road? You must have heard something, otherwise you would not be you. Your two ears hear more rumours in a single week than twenty barmaids would in a month."

"Ah," said Lestrange with a knowing smile. "Yes, there have been a couple of disappearances out that way, but it's mostly merchants making their way over to Riom to offload their wares who are being attacked."

"So, Guillaume is correct," muttered Caen.

"Beg your pardon?" asked Lestrange, scratching his rough sandy beard.

"It doesn't matter, continue."

"As best as I understand it, these werewolves are of the Lune Solaire affliction. They will prove to be notably more dangerous than your average run-of-the-mill lycanthrope, if there is even such a thing as a typical one."

"Lune Solaire?"

"Oh yes," said Lestrange, nodding fervently. "A particularly nasty breed whose curse lets them transform into their wolfmen states at will, but they are strengthened by the full moon rather than dominated by it. It is a strange affliction that is thought to have origin—"

"They're still weak to silver?" asked Caen, not wanting the history lecture that would have come had he not cut his friend off.

"They are still weak to silver, but you can also simply run them through with a sword to put an end to them. They bleed like any other beast and without blood, well...I do not need to explain that, do I?"

"No. You've told me all that I needed to know."

"Are you planning to kill the entire pack if they have the girls?"

"Not unless I'm being paid extra for it," said Caen, inspecting his nails for dirt. "You know what

I always say, don't you?"

"Do not go out of your way in case someone else will pay you to clean up the rest."

"Precisely," said Caen with a small clap of his hands. "That has always been my philosophy, has it not?"

"Yet you still end up going out of your way and breaking this supposed rule you hold."

"I do, do I?"

"More often than not and you don't seem to realise it, or if you do, you like to downplay it."

"I guess I'm just too soft for my own good then, aren't I?"

Lestrange furrowed his brow. "Reckless may be a better word to describe you, my friend. If you would learn even a pinch of magic, you—"

"No," said Caen bluntly.

"Not even a—"

"I do not have the time, nor do I have the interest," said Caen defiantly. "Magic is a shortcut for the weak. I have survived this long without it and I am in perfect health, am I not?"

"Every soldier is in perfect health until they face an enemy they cannot overcome," said Lestrange. "Need I remind you of that brand of yours that you rely on so very often?"

"The brand that's been seared into my skin? No, I had completely forgotten about that."

Lestrange sighed and shook his head. "Fine. I will not ask again."

"You will not ask again *today*," retorted Caen. "I'm sure you will ask again next week, then the next and keep on doing so until you die before me. I don't plan to have my soul separated from my body anytime soon, Lestrange."

Lestrange shook his head, dismissing the Hell Stalker's comments. "You are in need of gear then?" he asked, eager to change the topic.

"I am in need of gear," confirmed Caen.

Lestrange walked to the back of his workshop while Caen leaned on the counter, tapping his fingers on the well-polished wood. It was a quaint little shop in the front, mostly selling arrows, bolts and skinning knives for the local huntsmen, but Lestrange kept many special items in the back for customers like Caen who required a bit more variance for their targets.

Indeed, Caen has been using Lestrange's services for the past four years and found him to be exceptionally reliable. He was useful in many more ways than simply as someone to arm you, for he had a way of finding out all of the goings on in Bastia and the world beyond. Caen would ask him how he knows everything that he knows and Lestrange would simply say.

"I heard things."

"But where from?" Caen would ask.

"All sorts of people."

"Such as?"

"I'm a friendly fella and people talk to me. You would have more friends too if you were not so rude."

"I am not rude."

"No, you do not realise when you are being rude," Lestrange had said many times, "but I tolerate it because I know you don't mean ill by your words."

Lestrange returned from his backroom workshop with his arms spilling over with various weapons, pieces of armour and odd devices Caen couldn't even hope to comprehend. The shopkeeper dropped them onto the counter and spread them out with a satisfied look on his face.

"Is all of this necessary?" asked Caen.

"No, but you can have your pick of the litter for a reasonable fee," said Lestrange. "Now, let me tell you about each of them. We'll start with..."

*

Caen walked up the road, now armed with a crossbow, a small quiver of bolts and a long length of rope. Most of what Lestrange had offered him would have complicated things too much for his liking. Shooting from a distance and a swift pair of blades for close combat was all that Caen needed to make quick work of his hairy foes. Lestrange, of course, couldn't hide his disappointment that Caen had selected the most mundane of what he had offered.

The western road was quiet and Caen had passed no one, save for a single old man who he advised to make himself scarce. The green and brown of the grass stretched out for miles over the low hills before reaching the trees and the higher hills while the mountains on the horizon were too far off to be barely more than a faded image that drew so little attention they would go completely unnoticed to the average man.

The day itself was still young and Caen had no desire to see nightfall when werewolves could be lurking around. The shadows of a forest and the tight walls of a fort would obscure things enough without the added dark of the night. No, this was a job best done in the light of day as many of them often were.

"The outpost," Caen muttered to himself as a small watchtower and archway came into view.

Outposts like these were common throughout the roads of Roch, particularly in recent years when all manner of horrible creatures had started to rear their ugly heads. Sadly, most of these outposts were left in an unfinished state as the kingdom had been growing poorer and poorer with entire towns and villages being taken out over the last few years.

Caen remembered one particular town called Autun that he heard of from Lestrange. Two or three years ago demons invaded from one of the hells and slaughtered almost everyone in town, including the Outer Sentinel that had been sent to clean things up. When reinforcements showed up after their mighty paladin failed to return, they found most of the demons already dead and the paladin himself mysteriously buried on the mountainside.

"What a strange occurrence," Caen had said.

"Indeed," Lestrange had agreed. "They only found him because the paladin's horse had climbed to the top of the valley town, crossed the bridge overhead and waited by the unmarked grave. You can't buy that sort of loyalty."

Caen walked towards the outpost with one of his hands held high to signal a greeting to the guards on watch. He saw nothing of them as he walked through the stone archway connected to the tower and proceeded on down the road. With strange occurrences fresh in his mind, Caen paused and looked over his shoulder. It was unlike the guards of this outpost to not at least bid travellers a disgruntled hello to let them know they were free to pass without issue.

Drawing one of his swords, Caen walked to the door of the watchtower and peered inside. Suspicious as he was, his eyes widened when he saw what awaited him. Blood had painted the walls and floor a deep red and feasting on the remains of the trio of guards was a hunched beast with thick grey fur, itself splattered with red. Its fangs were dripping with both blood and saliva while its eyes were narrowed and ravenously watched the dead guards, even halfway through its meal.

The werewolf paused and his gaze drifted towards Caen who stepped away from the door as the wolfman's sharp yellow eyes came to rest upon him. Who would dare interrupt his meal? Perhaps this cloaked intruder was the next course, offering himself as a tribute to the superior being.

Slowly, the beast walked across the room as Caen leapt backwards down the steps and fixed his feet firmly on the road. Had this beast been the one that had taken the Legot girls? If so, were they resting themselves in his stomach right now? There was one surefire way to check.

The beast lunged recklessly, not realising just who his foe was. As it burst through the doorway, Caen shoved the tip of his blade in its side and wriggled it about as he pushed deeper. The werewolf howled and whimpered in agony as Caen twisted the sharp metal as roughly as he could.

He pulled his sword free, flinging blood and fur through the air and spilling the werewolf's guts across the dirt road, showing it no more mercy

than it had shown the poor, half-devoured guards. The werewolf tried to remain upright, but its knees were weak and was reminded that it was indeed a mortal.

Caen looked down at the writhing beast. It was no longer threatening, but simply a pathetic monster whose humanity was forgotten. For good measure, Caen thrust his blade into the wolfman's skull to make sure it could not pull together enough strength to take a chunk from his leg as a final act of wretched desperation.

He shook his head at the pitiful sight, walked up the steps and moved inside the tower to survey the full extent of the damage. The guards were missing entire limbs and chunks of flesh from their torsos while their armour was strewn across the floor, protecting absolutely nothing. It was a scene of the most abominable savagery and Caen would not wish this fate on anyone except for his worst enemies and, even then, he would only wish it if he was having a bad day.

Caen stared at the rays of light coming in through the narrow windows at the base of the tower. "Daylight," he said quietly. "Lestrange is right about this Lune Solaire curse. Oh, how I wished he were not, but when is that know-it-all ever wrong?"

Thinking that the scent of the wolf may be useful to him later, he cut large slices of its pelt from its body using a hunting knife he kept on him. The cuts were quick and rough, but he was able to remove parts of its fur and skin without too much blood being spilt. He wrapped them carefully in a cloth, placed them in a pouch and headed back outside.

Without looking back, The Hell Stalker continued up the road, knowing for certain that he was on the right path. For better or for worse, he did not yet know. The werewolves would most certainly be well prepared at their fort hideaway. If it was a particularly unlucky day, perhaps there would be other wolfmen who dared venture out onto the road in search of morsels like him who walked unaccompanied.

Caen walked for another couple of miles until he saw an outcropping of trees that opened in the middle to reveal a rough path. There was a set of stones stacked in a pile outside and the top one was engraved with an old rune that he could not read but he took it to be an invitation to the fort. Rather than take the path, Caen opted to walk amongst the trees where he would be much more difficult to spot; he hoped as much at the very least.

He crouched down at the edge of the treeline and cut a small length from his rope. He tied it around the pieces of the werewolf hide he had taken and slung it over his shoulder to hide the smell of human flesh as best as he could. He walked deeper and deeper, keeping the path just within his sight so he did not get lost while searching for the fort.

Surrounded by the thick scent of pine and with the pelt bouncing on his cloak, Caen wondered whether or not the werewolves would be able to distinguish the various overpowering scents from each other, but it was better to try and mask himself however he could. Knowing how powerful the nose of a regular old wolf was, he presumed the werewolves would be equally as good at this. For now, all he could do was make sure he avoided snapping too many loud twigs.

It was not long before the Hell Stalker spied the stone walls of the fort creeping through the gaps in the trees. He stood behind one of the thicker trunks and peered around, taking in everything. There were guards posted, but they maintained human form; this was good. Three loitering outside the front doors—it had no portcullis, excellent—and two more standing up top on the battlements.

The cogs were turning in Caen's head as he surveyed his target. He was always quick to formulate a plan, even if the plan was risky. Caen knew that he would need a distraction if he was to have any chance of making his way inside the walls and he knew exactly what to do to divert the attention of the guards.

He quietly moved away from the fort and gathered a bundle of the driest sticks that he could find. He piled them into a cone and doused them with some oil from a flask he kept handy. Pulling out a small tinderbox, he took his flint and steel, striking the steel against the stone a few times until a spark ignited the oiled wood.

Not wanting to be there when the fire attracted his enemies' attention, Caen moved eastwards and crossed the path once he was sure he would not be seen. After a few seconds, he checked over his shoulder to see if the smoke was rising—it was. He hurried along and waited behind a tree as close to the fort as he dared while keeping a close eye on the guards at all times. It would not be long before they noticed the fire and their eyes were drawn to it or they left to investigate. He would prefer the latter but would take either.

"Ey, what's that?" called one of the guards atop the battlements. "Lads, go check that out."

Perfect. As two of the guards below moved away to see what they could find and the others were watching the smoke, Caen dropped the unneeded pelt, slinked up to the edge of the fort unseen and looked around the corner. The last remaining guard on the ground was too fascinated by the rising smoke and the ones above could no longer see him. He moved quickly and quietly up to the door, pushed it—to his relief, it was not locked or barred—and slipped inside, closing the door behind him.

"Hey, who are you?" came a voice and Caen immediately whipped out his sword and thrust it into the throat of the man who stood before him.

"Bloody werewolves," Caen muttered as he pulled his blade free and the bandit slumped to the ground dead. "Step one had gone so smoothly, you cretin..."

There was no turning back now, he would have to move fast. If the girls were here, the cells would be the best bet. In a fort like this, Caen expected the cells to either be underground or at this very level. The entrance chamber was lined with hewn stone and before Caen was a narrow stairway leading upwards. No, that would not do; upstairs was the last place he wanted to be. To his right was a corridor and to his left another. It was a coin toss as to which way would take him to his destination in this old and musty heap of carved rocks.

Left. Caen hurried down the corridor, keeping a careful eye both in front of him and behind him as he moved along. There, a door to the right. Caen opened it slowly, a sword in one hand and ready to jump any creature that dared approach him. There was nobody here, but there *was* a staircase leading down. Could this be where he sought already? What a stroke of good luck that would be.

Caen closed the door, careful not to let it creak too loudly, and proceeded down the stairs, his second sword now in-hand. He could hear something; it sounded like humming. It was a low, but pleasant tune that reached his ears, growing louder as he reached the bottom of the stairs where there were three cramped, iron-barred cells all lined in a row.

There was a scraggly man with brown hair and a thick beard sitting against the wall of the furthest one, the only light coming from a flickering wall lantern. At least his captors had given him that much in this damp little cell underneath the fort, but the same generosity did not extend to his attire which was barely more than a set of large stained rags.

He continued to hum as Caen approached. "I didn't expect to see one of your kind wandering these sad corridors," said the man, unfazed by the sudden appearance of a stranger. "You wouldn't be so kind as to let me out of here, would you?"

"You wouldn't be so kind as to at least tell me your name?" asked Caen. His hat had no doubt given away his profession once again, but he liked it too much to part with it.

The man laughed dryly. "My name is Marius," he replied. "And yours, Hell Stalker?"

"Caen."

"Well, Caen, if you wouldn't mind indulging a man who has been bored to tears for the last couple of weeks, might I ask what brings you here?"

"I'm looking for a pair of young girls. They would have been here at some point over the last few days."

Marius started laughing again. "What makes you say that?"

"Why does that amuse you, Marius?"

"Amusement is a strong word," said Marius, ceasing his chuckling. "I would say I'm mildly tickled. Nobody else has been locked up in any of these cells over the last few days except for me. Those girls you're looking for? You're looking in the wrong place, friend."

Chapter 4

Unbound

"What do you mean?" asked Caen. "They have never been here...how could this be?"

"I don't know what you expect me to tell you," said Marius, shrugging and dragging his knuckles along the bars of his cell. "Would you rather I lied to you and said they were here and have since been released? When I say they have never been here, you should probably take my word as the truth."

"Who are you that I should believe you?" replied Caen. "You are but a stranger locked in a cell."

"Why would I lie? If I was a dishonest man then I would tell you what you wanted to hear, request my freedom and then betray you. So far, I've asked you to free me and then told you the truth at your own request, much to my own detriment in this peculiar situation I find myself in."

Caen kicked the wall in frustration. "All this time wasted when those girls could be werewolf food already."

"Werewolf food?"

"Yes," said Caen. "These girls were seemingly abducted by werewolves from their beds in the night."

"Is that so?" asked Marius, pausing to ponder. "Seemingly, you say? How is it that you are not sure?"

"I was led to believe that, but perhaps there has been a mistake."

"If there were two girls who had been gobbled up by one of those hairballs outside, I would have heard about it. Whoever took them, it was no werewolf."

"And how would you have heard about it? Do they make it a habit to tell their prisoners their secrets?"

Marius smiled a savage smile. "Those imbeciles outside don't know when to shut their mouths, such braggarts as they are. And I am one of them."

Caen stared at Marius with narrowed eyes. "You are one of the lycanthropes? You must have done something pretty heinous to wind up locked up in here."

"Heinous?" chuckled Marius, surprisingly jovial considering his current predicament. "They've locked me up here because I refuse to go along with their plan of abducting travellers on the road. For one, it is foolish and they'll get themselves slaughtered before too long. Secondly, I would rather not harm innocents if I can help it."

"How noble of you."

"I would say so," shrugged Marius, running his fist along the bars once again. "I was turned against my will and refuse to change forms because I know that I will not be able to control myself. My first transformation was a horrifying experience, not to mention painful. I was an animal, no longer human and no longer able to restrain my instincts."

"You killed someone?"

Marius hung his head in shame, no longer fiddling with the bars. "Yes," he said, his voice a mere whisper. "I feel the impulse to change, to feed on flesh, but I have continued to hold out. It would be nice to do so until my dying day, yet I suspect I will not have that luxury. The bloodlust will manifest in me as it does in the others."

"And yet you would still like for me to let you out?"

"Yes," said Marius. "There is a monastery in the mountains to the west. I will go there and submit myself to the monks. They may be able to aid me with my affliction or they may simply keep me under lock and key, but either way, it will be a preferable alternative to being stuck here with *those* creatures."

Caen watched Marius silently as a debate raged on in his mind. The man seemed to be quite forthright with him, yet it could all be a ploy. Even still, what Marius had said about Amélie and Celine Legot not being here...he did not need to do that. There was also the issue of Caen being able to escape alone, perhaps Marius could be useful in that sense. Even if he were to simply be used as bait, that would help Caen. It was a sad consideration, but the Hell Stalker could not ignore the temptation to at least think about it.

"Very well," he said. "I would like you to make an oath to me, Marius."

"An oath?"

"Yes. A solemn promise that you will go to this monastery and keep yourself isolated from society. It is my job to hunt all manner of monsters and creatures of the night, werewolves being no exception. I would prefer not to be hired to kill you because that means I am responsible for whatever trouble you would have gotten yourself into and any lives lost would be on my conscience."

Marius stood up and placed a hand over his heart. "I swear to you, Caen, that I will go to the monastery and turn myself over to the monks. Whatever they choose to do with me, I will accept."

"Very good," said Caen, looking around. "How do I get you out of here?"

Marius silently pointed to the far wall where a set of keys hung on a hook. The keys were of rusty iron and there was no more than a dozen of them. Caen rifled through them, looking for the one that would fit Marius's cell door. He tried one after another in the keyhole and found the right key on the fifth try. The lock clicked and the door glided open.

"Fantastic," said Marius, stepping out of the cell and holding his arms out wide. "To be a free man again, even though I am three feet from my cell, is a feeling like no other."

"Save your celebrations for whenever we are well past the forest," said Caen.

"Lead the way," said Marius, nodding towards the door.

Caen held up a hand to keep Marius quiet. He

had heard something from up above. It sounded like yelling. The bandit's body must have been discovered in the entrance chamber.

"Do you know a way out of here that isn't the front door?" asked Caen in a hushed voice.

"The roof," said Marius.

"To the front door, we go."

Caen and Marius walked up the stairs silently, listening carefully to the commotion above. The body had most definitely been found and the werewolves were on high alert. Perhaps this was the best time to make a run for it rather than wait to be found...or perhaps there was another way?

"Marius," said Caen, "do you trust me?"

"I don't really know you," said Marius.

"That's fair. Do you trust that I want to escape and am willing to bring you along?"

"Yes, I would say so."

"I need you to get back in your cell. Take the key with you so that you can be assured there is nothing dastardly afoot. When someone inevitably comes down here, I'll be waiting for them in the shadows, and you can attract their attention."

"Let's waste no time then," said Marius, hurrying back to his cell and taking the keys from the lock.

The werewolf locked himself inside while Caen stood behind a pillar, his swords ready for whichever foolish bandit dared venture into this prison. The two men waited and, sure enough, within a couple of minutes there was a rustling above and then the door opened.

Caen heard footsteps hurrying down the stairs. "Marius!" called a voice.

"Gervais. What is it?" asked Marius, doing his

best to sound alarmed. "Just what in the hells is going on up above?"

"Has anyone been down here," asked Gervais, approaching Marius's cell.

"Anyone?" asked Marius. "No, I cannot say that I've seen anyone. There's an intruder?"

"If you hear anything out of the ordinary, I need you to sound the al—"

Gervais's final words were cut short by a sharp blade piercing the back of his throat. He fell to the ground as Caen pulled his sword free. Now there was the matter of the body.

"Here," said Marius, taking his own key off the ring and throwing the rest of the set to Caen. "Throw him in a cell and do it quickly."

Caen did just that, locking the skewered bandit in the cell past Marius's and throwing the filthy tarp used for sleeping over Gervais's body. The moment he returned to hide behind the pillar, the door burst open much more violently than before. The descending footsteps were much softer this time and they almost sounded padded.

"Devereaux?" called Marius loudly. "Devereaux, is that you? It's hard to tell when you're so grey and hairy."

There was a loud howl and the wolfman leapt at Marius's bars and began to shake them vigorously. Marius said nothing as the werewolf tried to intimidate him, fighting to keep his eyes from moving to Caen who was waiting for an opening as the thrashing werewolf started to swing his arms wildly.

"What are you trying to ask me?" asked Marius.

"Where?" demanded Devereaux, in a harsh and grizzled voice.

"The intruder?" asked Marius. "He was here earlier, but he made a run for it when Gervais arrived."

There was silence for a moment, broken only by Devereaux sniffing the air. Caen was rumbled and he knew it. The Hell Stalker leapt from behind the pillar and swung his sword, but the werewolf turned with lightning-fast reflexes and blocked Caen's arm. He raised his other claw to tear the man apart, but Caen ducked and was only deprived of his hat rather than his head. He drew his other blade and slickly cut across the werewolf's leg, making the creature howl out in pain.

Marius furiously scrambled to open up his cell as Caen and Devereaux fought with steel and claw, the werewolf much faster than the man. Caen was struck across the chest by a swipe, leaving his leather armour torn and knocking him down, dropping one of his blades. Devereaux leapt on top of him and opened his jaw, lunging to take a bite before he suddenly gasped. He spluttered and coughed up a mixture of blood and saliva as Marius threw the wolfman aside with Caen's dropped sword in his hand.

"Here," said Marius, handing Caen back his weapon and helping him to his feet.

"Thank you," said Caen, retrieving his wide-brimmed hat and putting it back atop his head. "I don't think we've got much time before the rest of them sniff the blood."

"Then we run for it," said Marius. "We run for it and pray the scent of pine is enough to mask our escape should we be fortunate enough to remain unseen."

Caen rushed over to the cell where Gervais's

body lay. He pulled the man's sword from its scabbard and passed it to Marius, who gratefully accepted it. The two men bounded up the stairs and out into the corridor, where they were met by a dumbfounded bandit who had clearly been expecting Devereaux.

Caen kicked the man into the wall and stabbed him in the gut. Marius punched him in the jaw for good measure and the pair hurried down the corridor and back into the entrance hall.

"There!" called a man from up above.

The Hellstalker retrieved his new crossbow and aimed it at the bandit who was starting to transform before his eyes. He took aim and unleashed a bolt, which whizzed through the air and pierced the lycanthrope through the eye mid-transformation. The unsightly hybrid collapsed in death and Caen took a moment to reload his crossbow while Marius kept watch. Once it was readied, he slung it over his back once again.

Armed with their swords, the duo headed for the doors. They pushed them open and ran outside, where they were greeted by a half dozen foes—human and lupine—who eagerly awaited them. The two men glanced at each other and charged forward with their blades raised and ready to cut down their foes.

The bandits would not let them leave easily and fought back hard. Those with weapons made for Caen and those with claws made for Marius. Caen blocked and parried until he had the openings he needed, trying to play things tactically against multiple opponents. Marius was more on the backfoot, being much slower than the powerful wolfmen.

Whizz. Plunk.

Caen looked up and saw a crossbowman behind the battlements reloading. "Up above!" he called to Marius.

"I'm occupied," said Marius a second before he was slashed across the chest by one of the werewolves. He let out a cry of pain as they leapt upon him.

Caen ducked and weaved past the bandits he was fighting and thrust a sword into the back of one of the lycanthropes before hacking at the back of another's knee, severing its tendon and leaving it to crumple to the ground writhing.

Marius scrambled out of the way, bleeding profusely from his savagely-cut chest. Caen pulled a small silver coin from a pouch on his belt and shoved it into the werewolf's open wound. As he drew his bloodstained hand out, the werewolf let out a blood-curdling howl as the shining power of the mundane silver coin coursed through its blood and burned the beast from the inside.

Whizz.

Caen dove out of the way of an incoming bolt, which grazed his arm and tore his jacket. "We've got to run!" he called as Marius struggled to his feet.

"I...I can't," said Marius, leaning against a broken cart as the bandits made for him.

"Transform," said Caen, moving between Marius and the bandits.

"I fear that...I fear that I would kill you."

"I'm not so easily felled, my friend," said Caen, swinging his swords and blocking the strikes of his foes. He was then knocked to the ground by another wolfman.

Marius breathed in deeply and focused. He imagined the moon in the sky with its luminescent beams shining down upon him. Oh, it was radiant. Even the thought of it filled him with primal rage, long held back. Letting his willpower fade away, the curse of the Lune Solaire took effect and Marius began his transformation into a beast.

His shoulders grew impossibly broad, tearing apart his ragged shirt and he leaned forward into a hunch. His limbs and extremities lengthened and the nails on his fingers and toes grew sharp. His face stretched and he developed a snout as grey hair sprouted from his body, covering him all over. But what sent chills running down Caen's spine was not the hulking bestial appearance of his newfound ally; it was the look in his amber eyes. A look of bloodlust.

Marius pounced upon the werewolf that bore down on Caen and ripped his throat open with his sharp teeth. He turned to face the remaining human bandits who immediately began to transform into their own wolfen forms.

The Hell Stalker climbed to his feet and joined the battle, keeping a sword in his right hand and a couple of silver coins wedged between the fingers of his left hand. More bandits joined the fight from atop the battlements, armed with crossbows of their own while another half dozen ran from the keep, transforming as they approached Caen and the ravenous Marius who was feasting on the remains of the bandits, desperately craving flesh and blood to satiate his hunger.

Caen swung his sword, cutting the nearest werewolf's arm and then thrusting a coin inside the wound. The werewolf was crippled and dropped to his knees, shaking the needles in the trees with his pained cries. The horrific wails and whimpers made the hair on the back of Caen's neck stand up, but it was hard to feel any sympathy for a creature with such malicious intentions.

Marius meanwhile was beset upon by four of his lycanthropic kin, but his long-supressed bloodlust was greater than theirs and his control was much lesser. He was the deadliest of them all at this moment, now unbound by the restraints he had imposed upon himself.

"Go!" called Marius in a grizzled voice as Caen killed another werewolf.

"We can win this fight together," protested Caen. "We will see them dead."

Marius shoved the wolves attacking him away and leapt in front of Caen, taking a bolt to the back. The smell of another human up close was delectable. He wanted to open his mouth and take a bite, but he desperately clung to the smallest sliver of willpower that he had remaining.

"Go! Now!" he demanded, wanting nothing more than to feast on the Hell Stalker's flesh.

Marius dug deep and mustered what remained of his own dominance, repressing as much of his bestial instincts as he could. He stood up on two legs, grabbed Caen and shoved him towards the trees. Caen stumbled forward as he landed and looked over his shoulder as Marius was overwhelmed by foes. He could not simply let his saviour die.

Caen kneeled down with partial cover from one of the trees and pulled out his own crossbow. He took careful aim at the bandits above, firing down at Marius who had five bolts wedged deep in his body. Strong as he may be, all it would take was a single bolt in the wrong place for Marius's life to be snuffed out.

The Hell Stalker unleashed a bolt of his own and pierced the chest of one of the bandits, who dropped his weapon and shakily looked at his hands before falling out of sight behind the battlements.

Caen hurriedly reloaded and killed another of the bandits, who started taking notice of him once again. He retreated behind the tree he was using for cover as he prepared another bolt. He held his breath and leaned out, aiming for the gathering of werewolves piling on Marius by the front of the fort.

He fired and sought cover once more. A loud yelp told him that he had hit his target. He heard a bolt strike the tree he was concealed behind and knew he had taken a fraction of the heat away from Marius; exactly as intended. Marius continued to fight viciously; overcoming being outmanned by the other lycanthropes.

After leaning out and firing one more bolt from his crossbow, Caen fled into the trees and towards the road. The werewolves would not recover from this easily, even if they were able to kill Marius. If Marius won the battle, his human mind may be so lost that he would turn on Caen. The Hell Stalker knew that was why Marius was so intent on Caen leaving and he only wished he could have done more to aid his newfound ally, but he had a job to see through.

Caen did not slow down even upon reaching the road. He knew his scent could be followed much more easily now that he was free of the pines and needed to create as much distance between himself and the fort as he could. All the while, he was bothered. If the Legot sisters were never at the fort then where had they been this whole time?

Upon reaching the desecrated outpost, he finally stopped running. He was beaten and exhausted. Caen sat upon the stone steps and lay back, avoiding looking at the fly-infested corpse of the first werewolf he had killed that very morning. He must have lay there for ten minutes before he heard the clip-clop of hooves upon the road.

"By the True One!" exclaimed a man, no doubt having seen the werewolf.

"What in the world is that?" asked another.

"It looks like someone has taken its skin."

"That would be me, gentlemen," said Caen, rising to his feet and making his presence known. "You can thank me for it later."

The two men were sitting on a wagon, steering a horse down the road. They looked to be traders and they did not realise just how fortunate they were to have come here in the early afternoon rather than the morning. The look on their faces told Caen that they considered *now* to be the unfortunate time.

"A Hell Stalker!" called the first man who held the horse's reins.

"What manner of creature was this?" asked the second. "Why did you take its skin?"

"It's a long story, gentlemen," said Caen, "but I assure you that you do not want to continue down this road. This was a werewolf and there are more of them lurking just out of sight a few miles ahead. I would strongly advise that you turn back to Bastia until you've hired a couple of capable warriors to watch your backs."

The two men looked dumbfounded, glancing back and forth between the blood-soaked Caen and the mutilated werewolf.

"Why did you take its skin?" asked the first, wanting an answer to his friend's question.

Caen approached and hopped onto the wagon, startling them. He flicked each of them a silver coin. "I'll tell you about it on the way back to town. Just give me a moment to rest."

The two men looked at each other with their mouths ajar. The first man tugged on the reins and pulled the horse around. The wagon made its way back down the road and Caen held on tightly, keeping an eye on the path behind him and hoping dearly that no werewolves would follow them back to Bastia. If they did, well...at least he had some bait.

Chapter 5

The Boutaines Brothers

The morning sun shone through the window of Lord Legot's study as Caen stood before the lord and his son, Guillaume. He had finished recounting the tale of everything that had happened at the fort save for Marius's fate as he knew it. He had spun the story, suggesting that Marius had died before Caen made his escape. With any luck, Marius had finished off the last of the bandits, regained control of himself and was well on his way to the monastery.

"I do not understand," said Lord Legot, his two palms pressed against his face as he thought through everything that Caen had told him. "How could they not be with the werewolves?"

"I'll lay it out plain and simple for you, Lord

Legot," said Caen as Guillaume stared at him attentively. "If it was indeed werewolves behind the kidnapping of your daughters, then it was not these werewolves."

"And you are certain of this?" asked Guillaume, sounding frustrated.

"I would stake my life on it," said Caen.

Lord Legot stood up, walked over to the window and then stared out at his grand garden that stretched out before him. He had a pensive look on his face and he appeared older than when Caen had last seen him, a mere two days earlier. Each day that passed with no sign of his daughters was taking its toll on the man and it was clear just how deeply he cared for his children.

"Hell Stalker," said Guillaume. "If you're convinced that the werewolves are not behind the kidnapping of my beloved sisters, then who do you believe *is* the culprit? Where do we go from here?"

"I believe that the werewolf hair was a plant," said Caen.

Guillaume laughed derisively. "A plant, you say?"

"Not to confuse you, Master Guillaume, I do not mean it was grown in your garden," replied Caen. "I believe it was a ruse; a deception. Whatever you choose to call it, it means the same thing."

"Who would be so thorough as to plant werewolf hair of all things? What would that possibly achieve?"

"Someone knew that werewolves had taken up residence nearby and wanted them to take the blame for your missing sisters. Who would believe in the innocence of werewolves should they be asked? Who would even dare ask them? No, it would be a case of slaughtering each and every one of them while presuming guilt. Then your sisters would be taken for dead and that would be the sad end of it. The true culprit gets away with everything."

"A little bit conspiratorial, aren't we?" asked Guillaume.

"Perhaps I'm conspiratorial because there is a conspiracy? I am doing my job and investigating Amélie and Celine's disappearance and this is what it's led me to."

"And your judgement is so sound?"

"Need I remind you that these are *your* sisters that are missing, little master."

"Little master?" asked an affronted Guillaume, looking to his father.

"Enough!" barked Lord Legot, growing impatient. "Caen, you are to continue investigating however you can. I don't care how ridiculous your theory is if you can prove it. Do you have any other leads you can explore?"

"I do," bluffed Caen. "I'll start making those enquiries immediately. Rest assured I will do whatever I can to ensure Amélie and Celine are found. Have a good day, gentlemen."

"I will show you out," said Guillaume through gritted teeth.

"That won't be necessary."

Caen departed from the study and made his way out of the manner. He did not know whether Guillaume knew more than he let on or if he was always annoyingly sceptical, but Caen did not trust him either way. That said, after Lord Legot had previously told him that Guillaume was not a suspect he did not know if he could get away with prying further. He would have to think things through and piece together his next steps another way.

*

"Curses," said Caen, drinking his ale in the tavern of the noisy inn. "He's got something to do with his sisters' disappearance, I know it. If Guillaume isn't behind it, he at least knows who is."

"And you have no way to prove it," said Lestrange, sipping on his mulled wine.

"This job may wind up a dead end if I cannot investigate him."

"And what is stopping you?"

"The lord himself would not have it. Even if I were to prove that Guillaume has some involvement, I can't even be sure that Lord Legot would accept it."

"Can you not investigate Guillaume without the lord's permission?" asked Lestrange, staring into his cup.

"My friend, I still wish to be paid for this job," said Caen with a dry laugh. "Do you think I do any of this out of the goodness of my heart?"

"Sometimes goodness of the heart is a good enough reason."

"Very well, then I don't doubt you will give away all of your wares for free after this conversation."

"If I cannot make any coin, then I cannot buy more wares to sell in the future, therefore depriving the entire town of my services."

"And if I cannot make any coin, I will starve and not have the opportunity to slaughter the nightmare creatures that plague our land."

"Point taken," said Lestrange, finishing his wine. "I shall leave you to think things through, Caen. If you need anything, you know where I'll be."

"And I'll be there with coin in hand."

"No doubt," said Lestrange, paying for his drink. "I'll keep an ear out for you and track you down should I hear anything that may help your search. I presume you will be lingering around town for the time being."

"For the time being," confirmed Caen.

"Excellent," said Lestrange, putting his hand on Caen's shoulder. "Do not drink too much tonight, my friend. You will want a clear head to figure out your next move."

With Lestrange having departed, Caen sat in the tavern with a dozen strangers, all of whom gave him a wide berth. He knew that if he discarded his hat, he would look more like a regular mercenary rather than a Hell Stalker. He refused to do so, of course, being a man who was very proud of his role in the world. He was convinced that he would one day be able to show the people of Roch that he was a vanquisher of evil and not the one to summon it, wittingly or unwittingly.

"Another one?" asked the curly redheaded barmaid. She stared at Caen with a look of intrigue, leaning over the bar and exposing her ample cleavage to him.

Caen couldn't avert his eyes—not that he even tried— and downed the rest of his ale in a single gulp. "Yes," he said, slamming the empty tankard on the countertop.

*

Caen silently slipped on his boots and crept across the room, leaving the beautiful barmaid sleeping peacefully naked on the bed. He would have loved to stay until morning, but he had decided that there was no better time to sneak around Legot Manor than the dead of night. The security clearly was not so great if two young women could be whisked away without anybody noticing until morning.

The Hell Stalker slinked through the door and closed it silently behind him before making his way down the stairs. He walked through the now-empty tavern and to the front door that led into the street. It was locked, of course. Caen didn't want to risk waking his newfound bedfellow while searching for a key among her discarded clothing and decided the window was the best way out.

He clumsily escaped from the inn, pushed the window closed, and walked through the streets. It must have been at least an hour or two after midnight for the streets were almost entirely abandoned save for a couple of vagrants and drunks who were no doubt hiding from their angry wives.

Caen walked along for a short while and passed the familiar fountain that sat in the town square, ignoring the stragglers as he made his way to Legot Manor. He was grateful that it was not raining tonight for the last thing he wanted to do was leave muddy footprints during his infiltration.

"Oi!" called a man from the street.

"Yes?" Caen asked, turning around to see who had addressed him so impolitely.

It was a nightwatchman. "You better not be causing trouble around these parts," he said, holding his lantern high. He was a burly fellow with black hair and thick sideburns that ran down his face and into his beard. He had no moustache which made him look somewhat peculiar, but not quite silly enough to be someone you would dare pick a fight with.

"I'm simply heading to a friend's house," replied Caen. "I was having a few drinks and my friend kindly offered me a room for the night."

"Is that so, eh?" asked the nightwatchman, eyeing Caen suspiciously. "You're a Hell Stalker, aren't you?"

"I am."

"Then just know that I've got my eye on you, friend. If I catch as much as a whiff of demon in this town, I'll know it's you who brought it here. Think you can cause trouble and get paid to undo your own mess, do you?"

"Nothing of the sort, I assu—"

Caen suddenly felt an intense pain on the back of his head and fell forward as all went black.

*

Whistling? Who was whistling? This was the first thought that came into Caen's mind as he regained consciousness. He opened his eyes and all he could see was darkness, but he could feel the cloth sack covering his head. It smelled like animal feed. Had he been a man of weak stomach, he would have thrown up, but having been covered in the entrails of many a monster this was tame in comparison.

His wrists and ankles were bound and he could feel the rumbling underneath him as the muffled turning of wheels and a pair of horses' footsteps reached his ears. He was in the back of a wagon and he suspected this one wasn't taking him anywhere safe. He kept his head down and did not say a word, knowing that he would not be left alone here. He waited in silence for someone to speak.

"This sad sack is out for the count," came the nightwatchman's voice. Caen had the sneaking suspicion that he was not really a nightwatchman.

"Don't wake him, Marc," came another softer, but more sinister voice.

"Why not, Alain?" said Marc, the nightwatchman impersonator. "We've got him outnumbered and he's got no weapons. It would be fun to make him squirm a little before we arrive. What do you say, boys?"

There was a murmur of agreement. There must have been at least another three men here on top of Marc and Alain. What were those names? They sounded familiar to Caen, but he had never been good with names. Where had he heard them before? If they were going to wake him anyway...

"Lovely night, gentlemen, isn't it?" asked Caen nonchalantly.

Marc guffawed as he pulled the sack from Caen's head, revealing the back of the wagon. It was lit by a single lantern, the same lantern that

Marc had been carrying when he had distracted Caen. Free from his nightwatchman garbs, Marc looked much more thuggish. He was draped in dark green clothing and protected by brown leather armour that was covered in metal studs. He immediately drew further ire from Caen because atop Marc's head sat Caen's hat.

"Nice to meet you again, Hell Stalker," said Marc with a smug grin upon his face. "Sorry about the ruse earlier. I hope you don't hold it against me."

"I would never take a kidnapping personally," said Caen sarcastically.

"You shouldn't," said Marc. "Just doing business, my friend."

"Marc!" called Alain from somewhere outside.

"What's it matter, brother?" asked Marc. "Where he's going, it doesn't matter what we say to him now."

"And where would we be going?" asked Caen.

"Taking a little trip to a village called Lille. Lovely place this time of year."

"Lille..." muttered Caen, racking his brain. "Ah yes, I remember. That's the one that was overrun by the demons a few months ago, isn't it? Now why in the Outer World would we be going there?"

"Like I said," replied Marc, putting a hand on Caen's shoulder and giving him a pat. "It's just business, my friend. Shame really, I don't mind you Hell Stalker fellows when you're not taking our work. I've got a healthy respect for the trade, you know?"

Caen suddenly realised who these men were; Marc and Alain, at least. "The Boutaines brothers," he said. "I should have known it was you pair. Who are these other deadbeats? Your lackeys?"

The mercenaries in the back of the wagon with Caen and Marc looked furious to be insulted in such a way, but Marc Boutaines guffawed heartily.

"Easy there, fellas," said their boss, holding up his hands as they reached for their weapons. "We've got to deliver him alive, mind. We don't get paid in full if he dies before Lille."

"Who's paying you?" asked Caen.

"That's none of your business," called Alain from outside.

"I would say that it's very much my business if I'm the cargo you're delivering," replied Caen. "You wouldn't deny a dying man's request to know who it was that ordered his death, would you?"

"I would," said Alain coldly. Caen wanted to see the man's face so he would have an easier time finding and killing him later.

Marc shrugged. "If Alain says you're not to know, then you're not to know, pal. It'll torture you a little, no doubt, but I'm sure you'll forget all about it when we reach Lille."

"Are we far? I'd prefer to get this over with…whatever *this* happens to be. I'm sure it's unpleasant if you didn't just kill me back in Bastia."

"Job's a job," said Marc nonchalantly. "If I had my way, I probably would have just killed you there and then. If I'm killing demons, undead or whatever other nasty creature of the night it happens to be then it's quite the thrill. Another human? I don't like things to get too messy unless it's personal. In any case, no, we're not too far from Lille. It shouldn't be more than twenty or thirty minutes."

"And what is it that awaits us there?"

"It's less what awaits *us* and more what awaits *you*, Caen. I'd love to make it quick for you, but you're needed as tribute."

"Not another word!" roared Alain furiously.

"Easy brother, easy," said Marc with a look of fear on his face before turning back to Caen. "I guess we'll just have to enjoy the silence, eh?"

The wagon continued on down the road for a while before the sound of hooves on stone turned to a softer thud. The wagon wheels felt bumpier beneath them, yet they rolled more smoothly. Were they on mud? No, that would mean they'd be stuck. They must be travelling on the grass. If they were heading to a village, it was odd that they were now travelling off-road...unless the road was too dangerous to take?

"Stop," came Alain's voice from outside. "We've gone far enough. Any further and it'll be us too."

It'll be us too. That was the final confirmation that Caen needed about why he was being taken to Lille. He was a sacrifice to the demons that remained there. Was this also the fate of the Legot sisters? Perhaps it was not Guillaume after all, but the Boutaines brothers working for someone else entirely. In any case, he had his lead. All he needed to do was survive what was in store for him.

"Marc, bring him out," said Alain. "The rest of you wait outside the wagon."

Everyone climbed out of the wagon except for Caen, who was dragged rather roughly by Marc and thrown onto the muddy grass. Alain pulled Caen up and looked him in the eye. He was a handsome man with his blonde hair tied back into a ponytail and a ruffled shirt not quite fitting of a mercenary, but he had a reputation for being much colder and more calculating than his brother. Lestrange had worked with the pair before, and he had said that Alain was a fierce negotiator while Marc was the main muscle of their operation.

"I'm sorry it had to be this way," said Alain. "While we won't be able to retrieve your corpse from your death site, I will be sure to deliver your swords and crossbow back to someone in Bastia. Do you have a next of kin?"

"It's just me," said Caen. "Although you could give them to Lestrange. I'm sure he'd keep them until I get back."

"I assure you that won't happen," said Alain.

"I'll be keeping the hat," said Marc, flicking Caen's hat that rested on his head with a finger. "Fits me nicely."

Alain nodded to Marc. "Come, brother."

"A please would be nice, Alain," said Marc with a laugh.

"Do not try my patience any further," spat Alain.

"Men," said Marc turning to his minions. "Kill the lanterns until we get back. Don't want any vermin crawling out and destroying our ride home now, do we?"

The men snuffed out the flickering flames of the lanterns that hung upon the sides of the wagon while Alain and Marc each grabbed Caen under an arm and forced him along the path. It was humiliating having to shuffle his bound feet in such a way to keep up, but he refused to let them carry him the whole way.

As the three made their way through the nearly barren trees towards the town, a large bell tower passed by the shining moon as a dark silhouette. They were much closer than Caen had first suspected. The trio continued towards Lille, which was as silent as could be.

"Did your mother realise your name would rhyme when she called you Alain Boutaines?" asked Caen.

"Shut up," said Alain as Marc stifled a chuckle.

"Or what?" asked Caen. "They'll hear me, will they?"

Alain elbowed Caen in his ribs, which were no longer protected by his leather armour. He knew it was coming and tensed his muscles, avoiding being winded.

"Good evening, Lille!" Caen called out at the top of his lungs. He started to whistle, but Marc thumped him in the jaw.

"Quiet, you maniac," he said, no longer amused. "It's like I said, this ain't personal. Now shut up and face your death like a man rather than dragging us into it."

"That's not going to fly, gentlemen," said Caen, his jaw aching immensely. He breathed in and started to yell at the top of his lungs as Marc shoved his fist in Caen's mouth to hush him. Caen sank his teeth deep into Marc's knuckles, causing the burly man to wince and pull his fist back out.

"Let's make this quick," said Alain, grabbing Caen by the legs and upending him.

"You bastard," said Marc, rubbing his knuckles. He bent down and grabbed Caen under the arms as the Hell Stalker continued to make a scene.

He knew it was childish, but the faster he could hurry the Boutaines brothers along, the sloppier they would be. At least, that's what he hoped. If it hastened his demise, at the very least he would go out having thoroughly angered the pair. A minor satisfaction in his final moments.

The brothers carried him through a final stretch of trees and towards a stone wall that surrounded the village. It must have been about six feet high, far from tall enough to keep an invasion of demons out. Alain dropped Caen's legs and Marc picked him up and put him over his shoulder.

"It's been a pleasure," said Marc as he carried Caen right up to the wall.

The younger Boutaines brother had little difficulty in hoisting Caen up and throwing him over the wall. Caen's face was scratched by the rough stone as he rolled over and fell off the far side. When he hit the ground, Caen finally fell silent.

Chapter 6

The Iron Hound

Caen could hear the Boutaines brothers' faint footsteps fading away as he landed on the damp soil on the other side of Lille's wall. He rolled over to see the village and immediately winced in shock at what lay before him.

The houses were torn apart, gardens were a thing of the past and even the horses of the town had not been spared. Their equine corpses were but bones, picked clean by the demons that had taken up residence in this once beautiful little Rochian settlement. The demons themselves? Well, they were coming for Caen.

The three dozen or so demons had given up any pretence of resembling the villagers they had overtaken. They were all naked and hairless with their sickly green skin and their stubby little horns that protruded from the tops of their heads. They had twisted grins of sheer malice on their faces as they calmly made their way towards Caen who lay on the ground, his hands and wrists still bound. They were in no hurry as they walked, for they could see that the Hell Stalker was helpless.

"I had to shout and make a scene," muttered Caen, realising his folly. He had intended to make the brothers act rashly as they abandoned him in the village, but it seemed as though he'd only enticed the occupants. He knew it was a risk, but it had not paid off for him in the slightest.

Caen had to do something; he could not wait to be consumed by them. He refused to be a sacrifice, for he knew now that's what he was. He was a sacrifice to these demons and he swore to the True One that he would make whoever was behind this pay the ultimate price.

The Hell Stalker looked around, hoping for something that he could use to free himself from his bindings, but there was nothing. If he could use magic, even a simple fire spell, he could burn the ropes holding his limbs together and find a way to escape. He would not be able to fight back easily against this many foes, so entertaining that idea was pointless.

"Focus, Caen," he whispered to himself, continuing to look around. "The wall..."

The rough stone was the best he could do right now. He hurriedly rolled over once so that he was touching the wall with his back. He brought his knees up to his chest, shifted his weight to the left side and then manoeuvred his body so as to be sitting up against the stone. He pushed himself back and shimmied up, keeping his feet firmly planted on the ground. He was now standing, but he was still bound tightly.

Caen moved his hands around until he found the sharpest piece of jutting stone he could and then positioned his wrists in front of it. He started moving them up and down as quickly as he could, trying to cut through the bindings, but the demons were growing closer and closer. Thirty yards, twenty yards and now not much more than ten yards; he was out of time.

The demons spread out so that they surrounded him in an arc and closed in. Caen could feel the rope loosening slightly as he tried to cut it with the stray stands tickling his bruised wrists. The demons were fifteen feet from him. Looser. Ten feet. Looser still. Five feet. Almost there.

"Agh," he grunted as four of them lunged for him and pulled him away from the wall.

He was so close. He had almost done it, he thought as he was picked up by the four demons and carried away from the wall and towards the centre of the small village where a tarnished bronze statue of an exquisitely beautiful woman holding a jar stood on a plinth. He did not recognise the figure, but she was certainly no one he recalled from his knowledge of Roch's glorious history.

"Guresh hikyath kormoreth," cried one of the demons holding Caen. It was a horrid sound and made Caen shiver as the foul demonic words penetrated his ears.

The bell at the top of the tower nearby suddenly rang out. It clanged and it clanged, echoing throughout the entire woodland surrounding the village and the ground beneath the demons' feet began to tremble before growing into a rumble.

"What is this?" asked Caen as the demons smiled more sinisterly than ever. "What have you done?"

He looked around desperately for the source of the rumbling, but he could not see anything. What he did spot, however, was the sharp corner of the statue's plinth. It was a long shot, but it was his only chance to free his hands. There could be no room for error or he was most assuredly a dead man and the Boutaines brothers would not lose their heads by his blades.

Caen twisted his arms backwards. It was immensely painful and he could feel his muscles and tendons aching, but the demons continued to hold him tightly and made no further moves; they were used to struggling foes. He wrenched his legs from the grip of two demons holding them and then swung himself downwards. He slammed his feet on the ground and wrenched the demons holding his arms forward, throwing them over his shoulders and sending them tumbling onto the moss-ridden cobblestones.

The Hell Stalker hopped past them as other demons lunged for him, their spindly fingers brushing his jacket as he just managed to evade their grasp. He spun himself around and rubbed the frayed ropes against the corner of the plinth. A demon jumped at him, but he drew his legs back, leaning on the plinth. He kicked it away, sending the infernal beast into the crowd of its kin that were swarming towards Caen.

"Aha!" he cried as he pulled his hands apart. The ropes fell to the ground and he grabbed the nearest demon by the neck and smashed its face into the base of the statue. There came a crack and a squelch as its face caved in and spilt blood all over the old bronze.

The Hell Stalker tossed the pulverised demon aside and grabbed onto the statue's legs, pulling himself up. He reached out a hand, grabbed its arm, and swung himself up and onto its shoulders. He quickly reached down for his leg bindings and hurriedly untied them. The demons grabbed at his feet and tried to pull him down. He was almost free, but it was not over yet.

Caen leapt into the crowd of demons surrounding the statue and hit the ground with a thud. As one of the demons grabbed him by the arm and pulled him in, he wrenched himself away, sending his attacker off balance as he fled. He crawled between his foes and scurried to his feet, being scratched and bitten as he moved, but he was now unrestricted by the bindings the Boutaines brothers had so graciously left him with.

He forced his way from the crowd and hastened to his feet before dashing towards the nearest house. He slammed the door behind him and pulled the nearby cabinet down to block the entrance. That would buy him no more than a few seconds, but perhaps enough to find a weapon.

"Quickly, quickly," he said to himself, looking around the mess that was the desecrated house.

There were no weapons, not as much as a kitchen knife in sight, but there was a soot-covered fireplace. Caen ran over to it as the demons banged on the door. He grabbed a rusty old fire poker that lay on the floor, thinking that this would have to do for now.

Caen made for the nearest window when suddenly the glass smashed. He covered his face as the shards flew through the air, cutting thin lines into his jacket. When he moved his arms back down, he saw a demon smiling at him deviously from outside the window. Caen smiled back and thrust the poker forward, skewering it through the eye and wiping the grin from its disgusting face. He pulled his improvised weapon free, leapt through the window and was back outside.

The demons were onto him immediately and rushed towards him, keeping close together, but their movement suddenly ceased. The rumbling had stopped and, upon realising it, the demons turned to look at the looming tower.

The bell clanged one more time and a loud howl echoed throughout the night. What was it? More werewolves? Could he have been so wrong? No, it was a different howl. It sounded more like a dog; an aggravated dog. Caen ran towards the statue while the demons fled to the bell tower, but something huge was storming through the crowd and knocking the whelps aside without a care. And that same thing was aiming straight for Caen.

It was a hound, at least ten feet tall and far larger than any he had seen before. It was bulky and as hairless as the demons with skin so stretched that it was torn in parts, letting its bloody muscle peek through, surrounded by an orange glow like the fires of the hell plane of Za. Its eyes were as deep an orange as its glowing wounds and its brow was furrowed menacingly. Its teeth were as sharp as daggers, easily capable of tearing a man in two with a single bite. What told Caen that this beast was beyond an oversized mutt was the large sections of the hound's body that were covered by thick plates of black iron that had been grafted to its flesh to serve as armour for the nightmarish monstrosity.

"Keyl malak, Iron Hound!" cackled one of the demons as it looked over at its shoulder. "You will perish now, human."

Caen turned tail, running back towards the house, and then leapt through the broken window once more. He pivoted and faced the outside, pointing his poker toward the opening. He could hear the Iron Hound's savage paws beating against the soil as it drew near. He would wait for the stupid demonic dog to get stuck at the window and he would gouge its foul eyes out; a quick and simple kill.

There. He spied the creature barrelling towards him. As he prepared to thrust his poker at the beast, it tore through the entire wall, sending a cascade of broken bricks and wood into the room. Caen dove aside, moments from being caught by its jagged teeth, and he hurried to his feet as the hound reached for him with its paw as thick as his head. He ran to the front door, throwing the cabinet barricade aside and then burst through, dashing into the night.

Where could he go? He needed to get somewhere higher. He sprinted to the house next door, placed his foot on the window ledge and threw himself up as the Iron Hound smashed its way outside, making the house look like it had been built from twigs.

Caen scarpered up the thatched roof to the ridge, where he was furthest away from the beast. He looked around once more, hoping to see somewhere he could escape to. The bell tower was surrounded by the demons who were kneeling down and worshipping the Iron Hound from a distance, leaving the way to the wall clear. His best option was to make a run for it.

"Agh!" called Caen, stumbling back and almost slipping as the hound sank its claws into the roof and scrambled up.

The Hell Stalker ran down the other side and dropped to the ground, but the hound leapt over the roof and landed in front of him. It opened its mouth to tear him asunder and he shoved the poker inside, piercing its tongue. The beast yelped and recoiled as it bit into the rusted iron before swallowing the poker. It growled furiously as Caen ran for the town wall.

Caen moved his legs as fast as he could and he could hear the much faster feet of the Iron Hound pounding the ground as it gained on him rapidly. It was getting closer and closer and he knew he wasn't going to make it. He dropped to the dirt and the hound almost trampled him as it struggled to slow itself down before clumsily skidding to a halt. He knew now that going for the wall was a lost cause, for the beast was too fast and would surely be able to follow him through the forest. He had to find a way to fight it.

He ran towards the nearest house and jumped at the window, smashing through the glass like a cannonball. He rolled onto the ground and moved aside as the Iron Hound tore its way inside, once again sending bricks flying everywhere. Caen covered his head to shield himself and ran for the kitchen.

A knife. That was the best he could do. He

picked it up and hurled it at the Iron Hound before heading for the door. He didn't even have time to be dismayed upon hearing the clang of the knife hitting the hound's metal plating. He charged through the door and towards the next house as the hound followed, only minorly slowed by the sharper turns it had to take and the thick walls it had to break through, but it was enough to keep Caen alive, yet, he knew he was tiring much faster than his foe.

The Hell Stalker darted across the grass and into the house before him. At last, there was a weapon of actual use. A grime-encrusted old sword that had half been eaten away by rust was lying on the floor beside a table. He picked it up in his right hand, grabbed a rickety wooden chair with his left and turned to face the door. No more than two seconds later, the hound broke down the door and snapped its frame with its huge mass.

"Come at me!" yelled Caen, as the snarling and drooling canine stared at him.

It lunged forward with its jaw open and Caen swung the chair at it while stepping back. The beast clamped down on the wood as though it were a matchstick, snapping it effortlessly, but it was enough to give Caen the opening he desperately wanted. He thrust the sword at the hound's eye, but it jerked its head just in time and Caen skewered it through the cheek. It barked angrily and swung its head around, trying to shake the sword out violently, but Caen held the old blade tightly and the Iron Hound tore through its own cheek with its wild movements.

Caen stepped onto the table and jumped through the air with the bloody sword held high.

The hound barked furiously, its anger growing like an inferno as the man descended upon him. Just when Caen thought he was on the verge of the killing blow, a clawed paw beat him aside, ripping his armour and cutting into his body. He hit the stone floor and dropped the sword, which slid away from him.

The beast bounded past him and grabbed the sword in its mouth, biting down on the rust-eaten blade and spat it back at Caen in pieces. It had snapped as easily as the chair had and Caen knew his bones would do the same if he was caught in the hound's powerful jaws. It had seemed like a mindless beast to Caen at first, but it was much smarter than he had presumed. Yet, he would not let himself despair. He had to find a way to win. He must survive somehow.

He grabbed the handle of the broken sword that lay before him and pushed himself back to his feet. He ran outside, his legs burning as he tried to buy himself seconds to think in the hope that inspiration would strike him before he became dog food. What was left in the town besides more houses? The wall was a dead end. The statue? No, the hound could bite through the metal.

"The tower," Caen muttered as he ran, spying the crowd of praying demons surrounding the base.

Caen shoved the broken sword into his belt and ran without looking back, all the while he could hear the hound close behind him. Would it fall for his drop trick a second time? He had to try. Caen fell to the ground, then rolled aside; he was immediately glad he had thrown in the extra step upon seeing the Iron Hound swing its claws underneath itself, having anticipated the drop.

He scrambled back up and aimed for another house, leaping and climbing onto the roof while narrowly avoiding another swipe. He ran up and over the ridge, leapt back onto the grass and sprinted to the tower. As he passed through the open gate that lay between the spiked metal fences, he pulled the broken sword from his belt and held it out, daring the demons to attack him. He would prove to them he was as deadly with a broken sword as he would be with an intact one.

The gathered demons did not make any moves towards him. Instead, they continued their prayer where they threw their hands up and brought them down to the ground in a low bow. They repeated this over and over as Caen burst through the open archway and inside the small tower where all that awaited him was a spiral staircase of stone.

He started to climb and could hear the demons call out in their foul tongue as the Iron Hound leapt over the fence. There came the grim cracking of demonic bones as the worshippers were crushed by the uncaring beast. It bolted through the archway and Caen glanced down while continuing to ascend as the infernal menace stared up at him, thinking how to bring the Hell Stalker back down.

Caen was exhausted as he ran up the stairs, but he had to put as much distance between himself and the hound as he could. It tried to run up the stairs, but it was too large and heavy to fit upon the narrow staircase. It leapt up and swung razor-tipped paws at him, but it could not leap high enough to reach him. He had done it; he had bested the demonic canine.

There was a loud crash as the tower shook and

Caen leaned against the wall to keep himself stable. When the shaking subsided, he looked down and the hell beast was rearing up to ram itself into the wall a second time. It was trying to bring down the entire town to eliminate Caen and the Hell Stalker had nowhere to go but up to where the bell lay.

The bell. Could it work? Caen pushed himself forward as the tower was shaken again and again. It felt less stable with each strike, as though it was starting to sway even without the force of the Iron Hound's mighty headbutts.

He was so close now. He held the broken sword high as he charged to the top with his eyes fixed on the rope holding the bell in place. With three swift strikes, he cut enough of the rope away that it couldn't withstand the downward pull of the heavy bronze bell. The rope was whipped up as the bell plummeted towards the base of the tower. It smashed into the rearing hound's head letting out a short and dulled clang.

The tower was wobbling and Caen could see a pile of broken bricks surrounding where the Iron Hound now lay motionless with the bell half-covering its head. He had little time left before the entire structure would fall. He ran back down the staircase and leapt over the still-breathing, but badly bleeding hound. He charged through the archway and shoved his way through the grabbing and scratching demons who were infuriated by the defeat of the beast they worshipped so. Caen knew that even with a good weapon, he was not one for fighting crowds, so he kept on running.

As he made for the small gate, he stabbed one of the monsters with the sword and threw another onto the spiked fence, impaling it. The other demons ignored him and hurriedly made their way into the tower to pull the Iron Hound free before it was buried under the rubble of the quickly collapsing tower.

Caen ran through Lille unimpeded and straight to the wall. He jumped high and vaulted over it, landing on the other side. He bounded through the trees, leaping over roots and pushing through the bushes. From behind, he heard the crash of the tower vibrate through the air as it came down at last, but he still could not stop.

His lungs were on fire and his muscles were ready to burst, so exerted he was, but he must keep going. He ran through the wooded area and back to the road, yet he still did not stop. He ran until he could run no more and then dropped to his knees and fell flat on the mud.

Caen coughed and wheezed as he struggled to breathe. He had never pushed himself so hard in his life. After a few moments, he started to laugh through his coughing fit. He had done it. Today was not his day to die; he had survived. He had survived and he was going to find out who ordered his death and make them pay dearly.

Chapter 7

Insufferably Bold

"Are you alright, stranger?" came a voice from the darkness. The man's voice was concerned, yet wary, for it was not often he happened across stragglers sleeping on the road. He poked Caen in the side with the tip of his boot and the dozing Hell Stalker stirred.

Caen struggled to open his heavy eyes with the grey sky of the morning too bright for him to bear. The cool breeze on his face was the only thing that helped him stay awake, at least outside of the boot poking him in the side continually.

"Where am I?" he asked, sitting up in a daze and looking around. The question answered itself. He was exactly where he had dropped to his knees hours before.

"We're a little way out from Lille, but I wouldn't venture there these days," said the man.

He was tall and broad-shouldered, but he was soft in the face despite of his physique. There was a nervousness about him that said he would rather not be here, but his good nature compelled him to wake Caen. He was standing beside a brown-haired mare who was pulling along a small cart filled with sacks and saddles.

"What's your name?" asked Caen, forcing himself to his feet. His legs and chest were still heavy from their efforts much earlier that morning.

"Henri," said the man after a moment of hesitation. "Henri of Rudeaux's Horse Supplies. And you, stranger?"

"Rudeaux?" asked Caen. "How far from Bastia am I?"

"Bastia?" asked Henri. "Must be at least a dozen miles to the southwest."

Caen brushed his hair back and away from his eyes. How he missed having his hat to hold it in place. All he had to his name now was his clothes and even they had been torn by the Iron Hound during his battle—well, it was mostly a flight even if he didn't want to admit it—the previous night.

"Beg your pardon," asked Henri. "What was your name?"

"Caen."

"Caen? No family name or titles? Not even an occupation?"

"Just Caen is fine for now, Henri. Do not take it personally, I've had a very trying couple of days and I would rather keep myself to myself if you do not mind."

Henri looked mildly offended. "If you'd rather not share more than a single name, that's your choice, Caen. Might I at least ask what you were doing lying on the road?"

"Sleeping...apparently," said Caen. "I collapsed last night and didn't even notice myself drifting off. As I said, Henri, it's been a trying few days and last night was the worst of them. I wish you all the best, wherever it is that you're going, and I thank you for making sure I was not dead."

Caen walked down the road, determined to reach Bastia by midday. It would be a long walk, but his determination would see him through.

"Do you want to sit in the back and we'll take you a couple of miles?" called Henri.

"You would do that for a stranger who won't tell you more than a single name?" asked Caen, bemused by the well-intentioned merchant.

"Times are tough enough these days with all of the hellish goings on," said Henri solemnly. "I was paid a great kindness on the worst day of my life and if I can lend a hand to a fellow Rochian, I will do it."

"Well, it would be rude of me not to take you up on that generous offer," said Caen. "Only if it doesn't bring you too far out of your way."

"The road up ahead forks," said Henri, pointing in the same direction Caen had started walking. "The left fork will take you to Bastia and the right will take you to Autun eventually."

"Wouldn't know why you would want to go to Autun," said Caen, climbing into the cart while Henri pulled himself onto his horse. "If it has fallen once, it can fall again."

"Folks are trying to rebuild," said Henri

pleasantly. "It was a beautiful place before the invasion and we're trying to make sure that it is again. You can't wallow in misery, even when times are tough. If you don't push through, you'll give into despair and join the legions of the demons. That's not good enough for me. The world is never without hope."

Caen smiled to himself but said nothing. He watched as the trees passed him by, strangely calm in light of everything that had happened. It was nice to know that he was in good company. Perhaps he would find a way to repay Henri's kindness one day.

"Henri," Caen said, after a few minutes of silence. "Will you indulge my curiosity and tell me about your worst day?"

The horse supplier looked over his shoulder with a raised eyebrow. "You would ask that without telling me a thing about yourself? That's awfully bold of you, Caen."

"I'm a Hell Stalker," said Caen, daring to trust this stranger. "Me and my ilk are monster hun—"

"I'm familiar with people like you," said Henri. "They say you bring more trouble than you clear out."

"People say a lot of things, but what do you think?"

"If your kind were as sneaky as they say, you would have murdered me and taken my horse for yourself without a second thought. If you tell me you're a good man, I will believe you. Is it true that you're sorcerers?"

"No, it's not true," said Caen with a grim laugh, "but we are subjected to a sorcerous ritual as a rite of initiation. It grants us a few boons, but it also forever marks us."

"Sorcery is the quickest path along an infernal road. It taints the soul."

Caen looked up at the sky where a small sliver of sunlight was creeping through the clouds. "I'm no saint, Henri, I'm nowhere close to being an Outer Sentinel, but I do what I do for more than money. It pleases me greatly that I can kill demons and help people in my line of work, but a man's got to eat so I take the money that's on offer."

"Can't fault that," said Henri. "Funny you mentioned the Outer Sentinels because it was an Outer Sentinel who saved me."

"From demons?"

"Yes. I was a much younger lad, must have been around twenty-three years of age at the time, and there was a conniving witch who lived at the edge of my hometown. There were countless rumours about her, some true and some untrue, but it turned out that she had conjured demon lackeys to do her bidding. They were performing a ritual in a swamp nearby and I got this foolish notion in my head that I would be the hero of my town and kill her pet demons."

"Are you combat trained?" asked Caen.

"No," chuckled Henri. "That's why it was such a foolish notion. The townsfolk had called upon the Outer Sentinels to send one of their best to deal with her after we chased her out of town. Not a single soul was brave enough to approach her when she summoned demons to her side, save for me. I ventured to her hideaway all alone, armed with nothing but my cousin's sword and...well, I was captured and tortured for hours. Took my leg and everything."

Henri rolled up his left trouser leg and revealed a wooden pegleg strapped to the stump where the lower half of his leg once was. Caen hadn't the faintest idea, Henri's boot having been tied to the base of the peg. It was convincing and the merchant didn't seem to have any problem walking or riding.

"If I had waited until the next day, the witch would have been dead already," said Henri with a grim look on his face. "But if I had come earlier, I would have been demon food. Even the thought of that haunts me to this day. I still remember the looks of glee on the faces of the demons and the witch when they were torturing me; maiming me. Truly unrepentant creatures.

"When I had given up all hope of survival, a shining paladin with a blue cloak and a red-feathered plume rushed into the witch's hideout and slaughtered her demons before skewering her through her wicked heart. He freed me from the cage and told me that while he did not have the skill to reattach my leg, he could save me from dying of an infection. I told him to do whatever he had to and he sealed my wound."

"Who was this paladin?" asked Caen.

"Never did tell me his name, but perhaps I was too busy screaming in pain to have heard it. What I know is that he rode a palomino horse called Avalanche. I distinctly remember him whistling and calling its name after he had treated my wounds. Beautiful stallion, that horse was. The Outer Sentinel helped me onto his horse's back and he brought me back to my family. My brother helped me hop along to the inn to thank the paladin the next morning, but he had already left without telling a single soul his name. I haven't heard a word about who he was or a horse named Avalanche since, but I'll forever be in his debt and I'll certainly never forget his good deed for as long as I live."

"It's a miracle that you chose that day to be brave...or foolish, as you called it," remarked Caen.

"Indeed, it was," said Henri. "A real blessing from the True One. As I said, I would be dead if had I gone earlier and my family would have suffered for my folly. In saying that, had I not gone and the witch had been killed by the paladin, I would have gone about a normal life. There's plenty good about a normal life, but I've found a different calling and it's let me help others. The only cost was part of a leg, which is a small price in the grand scheme of things. See those supplies you're riding with?"

"It's hard not to," said Caen, elbowing some of them aside so that he could sit more comfortably.

"They're all gifts to the people of Autun. It's to help them rebuild. I have no doubt that they'll repay me with a meal and a bed for the night, but I have no expectation of that. I find that if you're good to folk, they're good to you in return."

"Never see a horse without feeding it an apple," said Caen.

"What's that you say?"

"It's a silly phrase my father used to say. He always said that if you feed a wild horse an apple, you'll have done a small kindness in the world and made it a better place. I didn't quite understand what it meant when I was a child, but perhaps there's something to it? Every deed we do sends ripples like a stone dropped into the ocean."

"Never see a horse without feeding it an apple," muttered Henri. "Wise man, your father."

"He was," said Caen. "I wouldn't be a Hell Stalker if it weren't for him."

"And what does he think of your chosen profession?"

"He never got to see it. He was killed many years ago by a gargoyle."

"I'm sorry to hear that, but perhaps his death spurring you on to become a Hell Stalker has saved many lives."

Caen and Henri talked the rest of the miles on the road until they reached the fork that would separate them. Henri offered to take Caen the rest of the way to Bastia, but Caen insisted that it was more important for Henri to reach his destination before nightfall so he wasn't travelling in the darkness. The two bid each other farewell and Caen continued onward to Bastia.

*

Caen walked into Lestrange's empty shop as the sun peaked in the sky. The small bell above the door rang and Caen glanced at it, wondering if the Iron Hound had been pulled free by the demons in time or if it had been crushed under the collapsing tower.

"Coming, coming," said Lestrange, wandering out of the back room. His eyes widened with shock when he saw the state of Caen. "What...what happened to you?" he asked, looking his dishevelled friend up and down.

"It was a rough night," replied Caen, only prompting a look of further confusion from Lestrange. "I met the Boutaines brothers. Absolute gentlemen, real friendly fellows."

"Alain and Marc?" asked Lestrange, rushing over to the door and locking it so they would not be interrupted. "You must tell me what happened, Caen."

The Hell Stalker launched into his tale, telling Lestrange everything from the moment he had left the barmaid's room in the dead of night to the journey back to Bastia with Henri. After he had finished talking, Lestrange nodded quietly.

"What is it?" asked Caen.

"The Iron Hound," said Lestrange. "I cannot believe they would summon it to such an insignificant village like Lille."

"You know of this creature?"

"It is not a unique demon," said Lestrange, heading into the back and returning a few seconds later with a large book that he set on the counter. "The Iron Hound a title passed down to a new beast each time the former is slain. Take a regular hellhound, imbue it with greater power than it ought to have, fuse its body with metal and there you go. I'm underselling the complexity of the process, but you get the idea. You're incredibly lucky to be alive."

"Yes, I'm aware of that," said Caen. "If I had taken any other action, I might not be."

Lestrange was flicking through his heavy tome. It had a black leather cover, and the pages within were old and torn, but it was densely packed with walls of text and detailed illustrations of the demons the text referred to. Lestrange had dozens of books like this, some of them preserved across centuries and at least two that could be dated back to the Dawn Era, more than four millennia ago. How they had survived for so long, even Lestrange did not know.

"What are you looking for?" asked Caen.

"The hound itself," Lestrange replied. "Aha!"

"You've found it?"

Lestrange rotated the book and pointed at a faded drawing of a creature that heavily resembled the Iron Hound, even down to the metal plates welded to its body. The text on the page beside it was in an old script that Caen did not recognise, but he had every confidence that Lestrange could read it effortlessly.

"That's it," said Caen, scratching his chin. "But the book doesn't do it justice. The brute was much larger than a regular old mutt."

"Yes, it gives a description of its size here," said Lestrange, tapping on the text with his finger and confirming Caen's theory about his friend's knowledge of the strange language.

"Why is it a concern to you that the demons would summon the Iron Hound?"

"Because the Iron Hound is a guardian. An enforcer. It is not a leader or a ruler, it is much too stupid, but it *is* loyal to whoever it is bound to."

"It is not a stupid dog, I promise you that."

"Did it or did it not end up buried under a tower that *it* knocked down?"

"That's neither here nor there."

"Do not get upset because a dumb beast almost outwitted you, Caen."

"I am not upset; I am merely stating my observations about its intelligence."

"Can you keep those observations to yourself while I speak?" asked Lestrange, clearly getting agitated by his friend.

"Apologies," said Caen, holding his hands up.

"The Iron Hound was first bound to an Outer World goddess named Elissar. She is known as a goddess of beauty, however, everything I've studied leads me to believe that she's a goddess of vanity. It is rather ironic that such a hideous creature is in her service, but I suppose the contrast between her and her pet makes her look even better."

"Is this goddess alive or dead?" asked Caen.

"Dead," said Lestrange. "She died a few centuries before the end of the Dawn Era. It's not known how she died, but there were many cults to her that followed in her wake and then were lost to time between the end of the Dawn Era and the beginning of our current Dusk Era."

"And who does this new Iron Hound serve?" asked Caen.

"It's hard to say," said Lestrange. "The moniker has passed between many iterations of Iron Hound and it has served many masters from immortal to mortal, from deity to demon, from demon to human. It would take me some time to research this and it would probably lead me to a dead end. These things are typically recorded in retrospect and after great disaster."

"Understandable," said Caen. "I would be surprised if there is a census for this sort of thing."

"Indeed," said Lestrange. "And what of the Boutaines brothers and their lackeys? It may not be the best look if you waltz into their houses and murder them in their sleep."

"Who would know?" shrugged Caen with his arms outstretched and a devious smile upon his face. "But I do have a plan on how to deal with them."

"You do?"

"Yes," said Caen, "and that's where you come in, Lestrange. I've got a huge favour to ask you on account of my current unarmed and penniless circumstances."

"How much do you need?" sighed Lestrange, pulling a small bag of silver coins from underneath the counter.

"More than that," said Caen pointedly and Lestrange begrudgingly brought out a few more sacks of coins one by one.

Chapter 8

Deal

"Lestrange, Lestrange, Lestrange," called Marc Boutaines as he strolled into Lestrange's shop with Caen's hat upon his head and his brother, Alain, following close behind and carrying three weapons. "I have some terribly sad news for you, my friend."

"Is that so?" asked Lestrange nonchalantly. "Is that a new hat, Marc?"

"It is indeed so and it is indeed a new hat," said Marc with a grin; the mercenary couldn't have been smugger if he tried.

Alain walked past his brother and placed the two sheathed swords and the crossbow he was carrying on the countertop. "I said I would deliver these to you," said the elder Boutaines brother.

"I'm sure you know who they belong to."

"Yes," said Caen, stepping out from the shadowed corner of the room, startling the mercenary duo. "They belong to me."

Alain's eyes narrowed as he turned and spotted Caen, while the hulking Marc looked utterly dumbfounded. Alain said nothing while Marc stammered something incoherent for a moment before falling silent.

"You're late," Caen told the brothers. "I'm surprised I beat you back here. Dillydallying at a tavern, were you gentlemen?"

"H-how?" asked Marc.

"It's a long story," said Caen with a wide smile, "but we have much more important business to deal with first."

Marc raised his fists and threw his left foot back while Alain drew his sword and pointed it at Caen, who held his hands up to show that he was not armed.

"You're not going to make us out to be fools," said Alain, a deadly serious look upon his sharp face.

"I wouldn't dream of it," said Caen. "That whole business about abducting me in the middle of the night...it was nothing personal, right Marc?"

"Right," muttered Marc, still struggling to believe Caen had survived and made it back to Bastia so quickly.

"Have you been paid for delivering me to Lille?" asked the Hell Stalker.

"No more than an hour ago," said Alain.

"Then that makes this much easier," said Caen. "You've received your payment and your contract is fulfilled, so you're no longer bound to your employer, are you?"

"What are you getting at?" asked Marc.

"I want to know who that employer is."

"You think we'd risk future jobs for you?"

"No," said Caen, "I'm going to offer you a job plus a bonus on top of that. The job is very simple, gentlemen. I pay you some silver and you tell me what I want to know. When I find the Legot sisters, I will give you a hefty cut of my finder's fee as a thank you for letting bygones be bygones and doing me one simple favour."

Marc looked receptive and nodded slowly, but Alain looked suspicious. "What are you up to?" he asked.

"Nothing," said Caen, nodding to Lestrange, who set a small bag of silver on the counter. "This is for your silence on my survival. Split it amongst yourselves or your men however you see fit. Marc, if you will."

Marc took the bag, pulled out a few coins and felt their weight as he jingled them in his hand. "It looks genuine to me," he said to Alain.

"Of course it is," said Lestrange. "What do you two take me for?"

"These," said Caen, nodding to Lestrange once more who then set two more small sacks on the countertop, "are for telling me who hired you to kill me. I don't need to know why; I just need a name. There's a bag for each of you and the coins are equally split."

Marc opened each bag in turn, checking a handful of coins. He counted everything and walked over to Alain, muttering something in his brother's ear that Caen could not make out. Alain let out a small sigh as Marc put the coins back in their bags and pocketed them.

"How many silvers are you being paid to find the sisters?" asked Alain.

"Three hundred," replied Caen.

"Per daughter?"

"No, for both."

"Give us two hundred and we'll agree to your terms. That's a three-way split between the three of us. Do you agree?"

"I don't have much of a choice, do I?" asked Caen. "I agree."

"Guillaume Legot," said Alain simply.

Caen's instincts were correct. Guillaume knew Caen was getting close and his bluff that he had leads to follow must have spooked him. The lord's son was going to pay, he would make sure of that, but Caen knew he had to make his next moves carefully. A single mistake could unravel everything, especially if Lord Legot himself caught wind of the Hell Stalker's intentions.

"Thank you, gentlemen," said Caen to the Boutaines brothers. "I'll be in touch once I've been paid. Marc, I would appreciate it if you returned my hat to me."

"I think I'll keep it," said Marc.

"You'll give it back to me if you want me to pay you your final silver," said Caen sternly. "If you're unwilling to do that, I'll be taking your head with it. Rest assured, I value that hat more than I value your life."

Marc looked unnerved by that statement, but rather than retort he flung Caen's hat over to him. Alain beckoned his brother to follow him and the two made their way over to the door.

"Not a word about my survival," Caen called

after them as the pair departed from the shop.

Lestrange started to laugh as the door closed behind the brothers and the tiny bell rang. He had been convinced that Caen's plan to get them onside would not work. It was ludicrous to even dare suggest it, yet the Boutaines' greed was greater than even he had imagined.

"You were right," he told his friend.

"Of course," said Caen, attaching his swords to his belt and slinging his crossbow over his shoulder. "I'm a people person, Lestrange. And you had the audacity to call me rude."

He had been fitted with new armour by Lestrange and he felt almost whole once more. All he needed now was to find the Legot sisters and get the six hundred he was promised. He chuckled to himself, thinking about how the Boutaines brothers thought they were getting an even split of the reward. That was never even a consideration.

"What are you going to do about Guillaume?" asked Lestrange.

"He thinks I'm dead," said Caen, "so all I need to do is wait and watch."

*

The rain poured down upon Bastia on this dark evening. The wind was strong and howled through the town as it blew the leaves from the trees and rattled the signboards jutting out from the outer walls of the shops. It was as miserable of a night as could be and Caen was thrilled that the conditions were so perfect for him.

He stood in the shadows behind a tree that sat at the bottom of Legot Manor near the gate. It was remarkably easy scaling the ten-foot-tall wall, particularly with rain obscuring the patrolling guard's vision so badly.

Caen had watched Guillaume return home that very afternoon from the shadows of a nearby alleyway. There was a chance he would not show his face again that night, but Caen waited and hoped that the young aristocrat would leave the comfort of the manor. If he did not, then he would simply wait until morning. If he did not appear in the morning, he would wait until the following afternoon. He would not leave this spot until Guillaume Legot left the manor.

The clouds started to roll away, breaking the seemingly endless pouring of rain that was starting to drown the flowers of the garden. The stars twinkled into existence in the sky, sharing just enough light to illuminate the damp path that led to the gate.

Not long after, the front door of the manor opened and a silhouette appeared, backed by the light radiating from the chandelier in the entrance hall. It must have been almost ten o'clock by now. The figure was no doubt a man, but was it Guillaume? Caen was not sure. The figure walked down the steps and along the path, covered by a heavy cloak and wearing a fancy hat, prepared for the rain to come back around.

"Are you him?" Caen muttered to himself, inaudible from the howling wind.

The figure looked over his shoulder toward the manor and Caen caught a faint glimpse of a sharp nose. It was Guillaume alright. He wandered down

to the gate and hailed for the guard to let him out. While the guard was distracted opening the gate, Caen climbed the tree and leapt onto the top of the wall. He lowered himself down onto the street and hurriedly moved into an alleyway before removing his hat, stashing it away so that his silhouette was not too distinct.

He listened closely and could hear the faint rattling of metal as the gate closed. Dare he peek out? He had to or he could lose his target. Caen pressed himself into the wall and slowly moved his head out of cover. There was Guillaume, heading this way. He pulled himself back in and hurried further into the shadows, watching the main street for the lord's son.

The clouds started to roll back in, bringing the downpour back almost as soon as it had vanished. The river would rise and overflow into the town if it continued for much longer, but Caen would not be deterred. He stood silently and unmoving, as though he was part of the wall itself.

Guillaume walked past without bothering to look into the alley. This could not be going much better. Caen moved back to the mouth of the alley and peered out to catch a glimpse the Guillaume. He was heading along the main street which would take him to the centre of the town before long. Just in case he deviated from the path, Caen would have to keep close.

The Hell Stalker pulled his hood up to shield himself from the rain and followed young Master Legot through the storm, even less than a shadow to the unassuming nobleman. Anytime Guillaume checked over his shoulder, Caen was nowhere to be seen. There were precious few people on the streets, most there by necessity from the occasional nightwatchman to the homeless trying to take shelter to get through the cruel night.

Guillaume walked into the town square, where the familiar fountain sat in the centre overlooking the abandoned cobblestones. He walked straight across and into a narrow street. Caen held himself back until Guillaume had disappeared and hurried across the square. He looked down the street just in time to see Guillaume vanish into a doorway halfway along it.

Caen walked over to the house as lightning flashed overhead and peered into the dull window as the thunder rolled in. There was a lamp lit inside, but Caen could make out nothing except for the heavily distorted shadows moving. The window had been enchanted and blurred. Why would that be? He stepped back and looked up. Would they be so reckless as to leave those on a higher floor unblurred?

The Hell Stalker placed his foot on the window ledge and leapt up, grabbing onto the higher ledge with his fingertips. He pulled himself up just enough so that his eyes were level with the bottom of the window. The proprietors of this establishment had indeed not bothered to use their magics to obscure the windows beyond the ground floor, although perhaps it would have been best if they did.

In the room was a large bed with a set of the finest silk sheets, but they were anything but neatly prepared. They were tossed to the edge in a heap while a man lay upon the bed with a woman on top of him, neither of them with a single garment covering their bare skin. The woman's long dark locks were braided behind her and swung from side to side as she slowly writhed up and down on top of the man.

Caen dropped down and back onto the street, preferring not to get caught watching the man and the woman engaging in their carnal acts. He was no prude by any stretch, but his kind had enough reputational problems to deal with and Caen being caught and accused of voyeurism would not make matters any better. No, best to stay out of sight until Master Legot had whichever woman he would use to take care of his needs.

The Hell Stalker slinked into a side street and sat on the ground; his already soaking clothes unable to get any wetter. He pulled his hood in more tightly and waited, his eyes fixed on the door of the brothel. Much like at the manor, he would wait for as long as it took until Guillaume Legot showed his face. This time, he would no doubt it would be baring a wide smile or a look of deep shame.

"Oi, mate," came a snivelling voice from behind him. "There a queue to go inside or do you take great delight in blocking me way? Got an appointment to keep."

"Go right ahead," said Caen, moving his feet in and gesturing towards the door. "I'm merely waiting for my friend to finish his business."

"Didn't ask, chum," said the man. He was bald-headed with a hooked nose and a permanent sneer on his face. "But seeing as yer explainin' that when I didn't care...perhaps ye've got something to hide?"

Caen stood up and smiled at the man, knowing exactly how to deal with this sort of character.

"What's your name?" he asked.

"Me? Name's Alvaro the Wise, also known as Alvaro the Bold and Alvaro the Slayer. And how about you, Hell Stalker? Oh yes, I've seen you about town before. Don't think that just because you ain't wearing a hat that I don't remember your face."

"Johann," said Caen, handing the man a couple of his last remaining silver pieces that he had been loaned by Lestrange. "And if anyone asks, Alvaro, you tell them the truth. I am waiting for you to finish your business with a lovely lady inside and we're going to grab a drink afterwards. Seeing as we're close friends, of course."

Alvaro gleefully accepted the silver pieces. "Feel like I've known you since I was a wee lad. We're so close my father woulda married you off to me sister if you hadn't started working as a mercenary."

"I'm glad we have an understanding."

"Likewise, mate," said Alvaro, pocketing the silver and smiling a satisfied smile. "Besta luck with yer business."

And with that, the sleazy fellow strode off towards the brothel door with the rain bouncing off his head and walked in as casually as could be. He was no stranger to a place like this, that much was obvious. Considering his ugly face, paying a woman for companionship was the best he could have hoped for.

Caen pondered what this place could have meant to Guillaume. His sisters were young and beautiful. They would no doubt fetch a high price if they were sold to the madam, but surely they would not be kept in the same town where they were taken from? Even if word had yet to spread widely that the girls were missing, forcing them into sexual servitude right here in Bastia would ensure that word spread quickly. Perhaps the owner had other brothels in towns throughout Roch, maybe even in the capital city.

Caen did not think highly of Guillaume, but would he do something as sick and twisted as to sell his sisters into prostitution? It *would* certainly earn him some spending money until his father died and he got a much larger share of his family inheritance upon Lord Legot's death. At the same time, Caen had the impression that the lord took great care of his children financially even now, so something wasn't adding up.

He exhaled as he waited, hating the thoughts that ran through his mind, but he had sadly seen much worse from demons. They did not shy away from torture, rape and murder. Those atrocities were what gave many of the hellspawn satisfaction. Disgusting creatures, demons were. To call them living beings was to put them in the same category as humans and animals, which was giving them far too much status. They were a plague in need of stamping out.

The Hell Stalker was lost in thought for hours, his eyes only losing sight of the door when he blinked. Many men came and went, but it was almost sunrise when Guillaume reappeared. The look on his face was a look of deep satisfaction, but as he walked through the rain to return home it quickly turned to shame. Once he was out of sight, Caen stood up and walked over to the door not wanting to give the woman who serviced him time to return to her room.

He rapped on it vigorously and waited for an

answer. A few seconds later, a young woman answered. Her hair was braided similarly to the prostitute that Caen had seen through the window many hours ago, but this one's hair was auburn, unlike the dark-haired girl from upstairs. For a split second, Caen thought the girl may have been one of the Legot sisters, but she lacked the freckles they concealed behind their powdery makeup.

"Do you have business here?" she asked in a stern voice that did not match her youthful face.

"It's an impromptu visit," said Caen, holding up a small pouch containing most of the remaining silver from Lestrange's loan.

"Come right in," said the woman much more softly, placing her hand upon Caen's cheek and planting a kiss on him.

He tried his best not to recoil as she took his hand, for he knew what her hands had likely been touching minutes prior. The woman pulled him inside before closing the door behind them.

Chapter 9

The Daughters of Elissar

The young prostitute locked the door to the brothel with one hand, all the while keeping the fingers of her other hand interlocked with Caen's. She turned to face him and caressed his face with a look of endearment; a look that she had used to sway many men.

"You are soaked, shall I take your clothes or would you prefer another girl?" she asked.

"You are perfect for me," said Caen, looking around the room. It was a narrow hallway with a wooden staircase leading upstairs, and a back passageway with many other doors where other girls were no doubt servicing clients.

"What is your name?" Caen asked. Upon looking into her crystalline blue eyes, he could see how captivating she was.

"Leticia," she said softly. "And you, my lord?"

"That is a beautiful name, Leticia. You can call me Johann," replied Caen.

"My lord, Johann," said Leticia, gesturing toward the stairs. "Shall I lead the way?"

"If you would be so kind," said Caen.

Leticia guided him up the stairs by the hand to another corridor of doors. She walked along to the third door on the left and opened it. She and Caen moved inside to the faintly and flickeringly lit room where there was a bed covered in the same fine silk sheets the Hell Stalker had spied through the window outside.

Caen had thought long and hard about how to uncover Guillaume Legot's business in the brothel. The nobleman had been here for far too long to have simply spent the night with a courtesan. No, he had been running his mouth at the very least or was dealing with business matters regarding his sisters at the worst.

Leticia began to undress Caen while he stood in the room with countless thoughts and theories running through his head. She caressed his arms and chest as she did so, almost wrapping herself around him to replace the clothes she was taking away.

"You are so strong, Lord Johann," she said in a hushed voice, resting her soft hands upon Caen's muscular arms. "Yet you are so scarred."

"I have seen many battles," Caen told her, "but each and every one was worth it to lay eyes upon a face as beautiful as yours."

She was indeed a beautiful girl, but Caen cared nothing for her. He just needed her to be receptive enough to start talking and considering the mixture of wispy and fat men that he had watched stroll through the doors, he was confident that he could win her over.

"This one," said Leticia, running her hand over a scar on Caen's left shoulder in the shape of a seven-point star. "It's different to the others. Where did you get this one?"

"It's a relic from a past life," said Caen, distracting Leticia by untying the bow top of her dress, which fell down and exposed her breasts. "Now where were we?"

Leticia pressed herself against Caen but kept one hand upon the star brand. "It is such a fascinating shape," she said, tracing its outline with her fingers. "It's almost magical, my lord. Will you tell me about your past life so that I may get to know you better?"

Something was wrong. She recognised the symbol. She should not recognise the symbol, for it was the emblem of the Hell Stalkers that signified being accepted into the organisation; an average person would have not have known it. Prostitutes hear many things, no doubt, but to know of the Hell Stalkers brand? It did not make sense.

Caen had to try one more time to distract her. He placed his hands under Leticia's legs and lifted her up, throwing her onto the bed. He climbed on top of her, but her fingers were again drawn back to the symbol that she was so fixated on. She knew; there was no doubt in Caen's mind. His seduction plan had gone by the wayside so he would have to take a more direct approach.

"Leticia," said Caen, pinning her down, but not

too forcefully.

"Yes, my lord," she said without taking her eyes off the brand.

"Why was Guillaume Legot here?"

Leticia froze for a second before pulling her arms free from Caen and reaching over the edge of the bed into the shadows where the flickering light did not reach. She fumbled around for a dagger and thrust it at Caen, who caught her arm with ease. She struggled against him, but he was much stronger than she was and she made no ground.

"I will ask again, Leticia," said Caen calmly with a smile on his face. "Why was Guillaume Legot here? Was he with you?"

Leticia had a look of fury upon her face, but it suddenly softened again and her face returned to a look of feigned innocence as she dropped the dagger. "My lord, Johann," she said, wrapping her legs around Caen's back. "I wish for nothing more than to please you."

"A little late for that, succubus," said Caen, pulling himself free and throwing the prostitute to the ground.

As she rolled across the floor, her face changed once again. The look of fury returned, but this time she bore two sharp horns on her head. A sleek, thin tail with a spear-like tip emerged from under the lower half of her dress and her nails grew long and sharp. The illusion had faded and Leticia's true form was revealed.

Caen leapt at her from the bed and pinned her down. "Answer me!" he demanded, as she whipped him with her tail, cutting into his bare back.

"Die, Hell Stalker," she said, her voice now harsh and warbling with all veneer of sweetness and innocence gone. Even her blue eyes had turned a harsh yellow and the pupils had lengthened into vertical slits.

Leticia threw Caen aside and sprung to her feet, but before she could attack him, he rolled over, retrieved one of his swords from his discarded belt and swung it up, stopping dead with the tip at her throat. She looked at him as though she wanted to tear open his neck with her teeth, but she dared not move in case the sword resting upon her throat suddenly impaled her.

"Care to talk now, servant of V'andrya?" asked Caen. He had encountered demons like her before, servants of the goddess of lust. Foul and wretched creatures that captured hearts with deceit and by preying on primal urges.

"I will tell you nothing," she said.

Caen shrugged his shoulders and lunged forward, impaling her through the throat. He placed his foot on her stomach and pushed her back, drawing his slinking sword out and leaving Leticia's body to fall to the floor.

The door burst open and in strode a woman in a long scarlet dress. Upon seeing Leticia's half-dressed, demonic corpse and Caen, naked as the day he was born, she screamed. The Hell Stalker held his sword away from her and held one hand up to try and quiet her.

"If you are not a demon, then I mean you no harm," he said to the terrified woman. "Are you the madam here?"

"Y-y-yes," she stammered. The look of fear on her face appeared genuine. "Is that...is that Leticia?"

"Yes," said Caen, still wary even though he

believed the madam to be a human. "You did not know of her true form, did you?"

"No!" yelled the madam. "I did not. I swear it!"

"You will tell me everything I need to know and word will not get around town that you've been housing demons, wittingly or unwittingly. Are we in agreement?"

Caen could hear other doors opening as the madam screamed.

"Everything alright, Madam?" came Alvaro's snivelling voice from the hallway.

"Yes," she replied, leaning into the corridor. "I thought this room was unoccupied, that is all. And I...I saw a rather unorthodox act that took me by surprise. No...no cause for alarm, please return to your rooms."

"Are you sure?" came another man's voice.

"She's sure," said Caen.

"Ah, is that my good friend, Johann?" asked Alvaro with a chuckle.

"I got bored waiting for you, my friend," replied Caen, forgetting the ugly man's name.

"Up to your usual tricks, eh mate? False alarm, ladies and gents. Walked in on him with one of his lady friend's once myself and had to scrub the old eyes with soap for an hour."

The patrons closed their doors, having been convinced that it was a misunderstanding and the madam turned to Caen who was glad that his earlier bribe had not gone to waste.

"Yes," she said, her face white as snow as she closed the door. "We are in agreement."

"First things first," said Caen, reaching for his undergarments. "Who was that girl? Had she been working here for long?"

"No," said the madam. "She came from another organisation a few months ago. She seemed perfectly lovely and willing to work, so we took her in. She has never given us a single problem until now..."

"And Guillaume Legot was a regular guest of hers?"

The madam hesitated. "Legot..."

"Do not play the fool," said Caen, fastening his belt. "It will not work on me. Everyone in this town knows of the Legot family."

"Yes," she said with a sigh. "Yes, the lord's son comes here a few times per week."

"I see...and where was it that she came from?"

"She came from Lille before...well, before it was attacked. She said her group was called...what was it now..."

"This is important, please think."

"The Daughters of...something. The Daughters of Elsewhere?"

"The Daughters of Elissar?" asked Caen, remembering the name from Lestrange's book. Elissar was the Outer World goddess who had bound the Iron Hound to her.

"Yes! Yes, that was it."

"And did anybody else come with her? Are there others of her group that you took in?"

The madam looked terrified upon Caen asking this question. "Yes, there are three others."

Caen finished getting dressed by throwing on his still-soaked cloak. "I suggest you invest in extra security, madam," he said. "Yours is severely lacking. Perhaps check in with the Hell Stalkers considering foul creatures are involved. If you can't find one for a reasonable price, perhaps even those Boutaines brothers would be able to assist you?"

"You won't help me?"

"I have other business to attend to," said Caen, moving toward the door, "but I wish you all the best. Perhaps you should pray to the True One, but I suspect he does not look kindly upon this establishment."

The madam put her hand upon Caen's arm as he opened the door. "Please, won't you do something?"

"I *am* doing something," said Caen, not looking back as he departed from the room.

*

"The Daughters of Elissar," muttered Lestrange repeatedly, pouring through a pile of books.

"And you're sure it doesn't ring any bells?" asked Caen as he leaned against the counter.

"You expect me to remember everything in my books?" asked Lestrange without looking up.

"You remembered the Iron Hound."

"A lucky coincidence as I had reread that text only last year. The pages of the book are starting to crumble so I was sure to take everything in so as not to open it again and ruin such a valuable vault of knowledge."

"This is going to take forever."

"It is incredibly fortunate for you that you are not dead," said Lestrange. "A demon of lust laid her lips upon you and you escaped by the skin of your teeth."

"I was under no threat."

"Purely thanks to your Hell Stalker brand. Had her magic been stronger, even that would not have kept you immune to her power to enthral and enslave."

"Yes, yes," said Caen, loathe to admit that Lestrange was right. "You are correct and you are far wiser than I, Lestrange. Now would you please keep looking."

"Of course," said Lestrange quietly.

"A small village like Lille having a brothel is a ludicrous notion..."

Caen tapped on the countertop impatiently as Lestrange continued to mutter and flick through the books. This took considerably longer for the books that didn't have the courtesy to include a table of contents or a glossary and even longer for the ones that didn't include those and were also in a foreign or ancient script.

"Ah!" exclaimed Lestrange after some time.

"The Daughters of Elissar?" asked Caen, alerted from a daydream.

"Yes," said Lestrange, holding up a pristine book. "This is one of my newer texts that I have yet to read in full. I bought it from a trader who passed through town after fleeing Altburg. He said something about King Gerath's overreach was star—"

"Is this important?"

"No, but Altburg is fascinating."

"To you."

"To many who are not you. It is one of the oldest still-standing cities across the Outer World, but perhaps not for long if King Gerath continues to run it into the ground."

"Do you know what *is* fascinating to me?"

"I do," sighed Lestrange before looking back to his book. "It says here that the Daughters of Elissar are a group whose founding members are descended from the deceased goddess herself. Whether that's true or not, I cannot say, but they seek to live up to her image and keep themselves youthful and beautiful forever by partaking in a ritual called the life feast."

"The life feast?"

"How does that work?"

"It's light on detail, I'm afraid."

"What sort of useless book is this?" asked a frustrated Caen, spinning the book around and inspecting it closely.

"It's not a specialised text," said Lestrange angrily, closing the book and shaking it at the Hell Stalker. If he had been a less patient man, he would have smacked Caen across the head with it. "We're lucky that it mentions the Daughters of Elissar at all, so you should stop besmirching it so carelessly."

Caen fought hard to not roll his eyes, knowing that it might have pushed Lestrange over the edge. "Does it say how to kill them?"

"No, but I have no doubt a sword or a bolt through the head would do rightly. Failing that, fire is usually a good option. The daughters may be human, they may be demon."

"Or a hellhound coated in iron."

"The Iron Hound is not one of the daughters, you fool. For a start, he's a male. Secondly, he's a servant demon and unable to speak. He does not participate in rituals."

Caen stretched back and then reached into the

air. "The Legot sisters must have been offered up by Guillaume. A sacrifice in exchange for whatever debauchery he wants to get up to, the sleaze. Perhaps he desires a forever youthful wife or a demon wench upon his arm like that enchanting little harlot, Leticia."

"That would make sense," said Lestrange, nodding along. "I would wager that the Legot girls are still alive. The ritual is only conducted on the tenth night of each month."

"What date is it today?" asked Caen.

"The tenth."

Caen sighed deeply. "It's ten o'clock in the morning. How could I possibly find the..."

"What is it?" asked Lestrange as Caen trailed off.

"I know where the ritual site is," said Caen, his face pale. "How could I be so stupid? The Iron Hound. Leticia. It's in Lille. There was a large statue of a woman in the centre of town. She was astonishingly beautiful and I would bet my right arm that it's a statue of Elissar."

"Was she holding a jar?"

"I'm not sure, I think...yes. Yes, she was!"

"Can you make it to Lille in time?"

"On foot, just about, but the journey would exhaust me. I'll need a horse."

"Why you insist on travelling everywhere on foot, I have never understood."

Caen smiled deviously at Lestrange. "I need a favour, my friend."

"You owe me more than enough silver as is, Caen! I will go out of business if you fail...I may even have to sell my books."

"No, it's a different favour, Lestrange. I have an

idea as to how I may be able to arrange for free transport and prove Guillaume Legot's involvement in all of this."

"And what do you propose?" asked Lestrange, eyeing Caen suspiciously.

"We're going to summon the power of a good rumour, Lestrange," he said. "The power of a good rumour."

Chapter 10

A Lost Name

Caen stood patiently at the outskirts of Bastia, cloaked by the shadow of a low stone wall that he waited behind. He prayed that his plan would work otherwise Lestrange would have him hung for wasting his money.

His plan was rather simple, he had spread the word around town that he was on his way to Lille, armed to the teeth, and ensured that these rumours would reach Guillaume Legot, dropping silver into the laps of those who were the mouthiest of all. All Caen needed was for the lord's son to act rashly.

Many had travelled along the road in this afternoon, but Guillaume was nowhere to be seen. Every time Caen heard hooves clopping against the stone or the rolling wheels of a wagon, he felt a small jitter of excitement only for it to be squashed upon seeing a merchant or an envoy riding along.

"Quickly now," came a voice as yet more hooves and their following wagon approached his hiding spot.

"Last chance," Caen muttered to himself, waiting for the moment to look out.

If Guillaume wasn't on his way, he would have to head back to Bastia, pick up a horse and make his way to Lille alone. He may still be able to rescue Amélie and Celine, but the slippery son of the lord would no doubt escape the fate he deserved.

The two horses trotted past much more briskly, but it was not a simple wagon that was being pulled along behind. It was a much grander carriage and emblazoned on the side of it was the Legot family crest. The curtains were pulled across the windows which meant only one thing, Guillaume Legot was inside and on his way to Lille to warn the Daughters of Elissar about Caen's arrival.

Now was his chance. Caen ran from behind the wall and leapt onto the back of the carriage, sinking his fingers into a thin bar of wood beneath the window. He kept low, watching the glass above to ensure that Guillaume did not stir. Once he was sure things were quiet, he reached up and grabbed onto the edge of the roof and nimbly pulled himself onto it. He could see the back of the driver's head and it was only a matter of time before he was spotted.

Caen pulled out one his swords and crept forward. He flipped it around, reached out towards the unsuspecting driver and struck him on the back of the head with the pommel of his weapon.

He quickly slipped onto the seat beside the dazed driver, snatched the reins from him and booted him from the wagon, knocking him to the side of the road where he lay unmoving as Caen continued to guide the horse along.

"He'll be fine," the Hell Stalker whispered to himself before checking over his shoulder. "A traveller will find him before the hour is up."

The first of the many hard parts was over, as long as Guillaume kept those curtains shut. The second hard part would be what came after he reached Lille. Caen had run around that village like a headless chicken as he fled from the Iron Hound and had seen no ritual, which meant that the site was likely concealed somewhere.

He was kicking himself somewhat for not killing more of the demon whelps as he fled, but at least the dreaded dog would pose no further threat to him. The whelps wouldn't have been able to pull it free before the tower collapsed; it was much too heavy.

The day rolled along without as much as a sigh from Guillaume Legot. Caen had started to wonder if the young master was even inside the carriage, but he laughed quietly to himself about his own paranoia. There would be no need for closed curtains if he was not inside.

Almost two hours later, Caen spied the road leading through the small, wooded area toward Lille. He awkwardly steered the horses onto the path and they continued forward. He looked at the wagon tracks that veered off the path and thought bitterly about how the Boutaines brothers had tried to drag him to his death. To have been forced to make a deal with them was shameful, but Caen would get them back one day and he would make sure that that one day was sooner rather than later.

Once they reached the iron gate nestled between the walls of the village, Caen tugged on the horses' reins to make them stop. He could see the demons gathered around the statue of Elissar and did not as much as acknowledge the presence of a carriage. He had no doubt that would change upon entering proceeding through the gate.

Caen could hear some shuffling from within the carriage and, a moment later, the door clicked as it was unlocked from within. There was no movement for a few seconds before it swung open and Guillaume emerged, hopping onto the path and then walking to the gate.

"Clement, I will speak to my father about you not bothering to open my door for me," said the lord's son without looking back to see who was sitting in the driver's seat and who had been steering the horses this entire time.

Caen slinked away and quietly hid behind a tree as Guillaume stood at the gates waiting. He looked through the bars and then finally turned back to face the carriage.

"Clement?" he asked upon seeing the driver's seat empty. "Clement?" he said again, sounding unnerved.

Caen stayed silent as Guillaume tepidly approached the carriage. He looked inside and all around it, alarmed to be standing here alone. He shakily pulled out a sword and held it out, jittering around and rapidly turning in different directions as though he expected something to jump out at him.

"Clement, I was j-j-joking," he said. "I will not

utter a word to my f-f-father about the door. In f-f-fact, I think you deserve a pay rise. Would you like that? Just cease this tomfoolery and come back here right away."

The gate suddenly clanked and Guillaume leapt out of his skin. He spun around and swung his sword wildly at the air. Caen peered around the tree and could see a woman in white robes. He could not make out her face except for her pure and pale skin along with her soft pink lips. He could tell that she would be stunningly beautiful from that alone. She was almost enchanting to gaze upon, but he would fall for no run-of-the-mill enchantments.

"Have I startled you, my dear?" she asked Guillaume soothingly.

The nobleman put his sword away and straightened himself up. "I am fine, my love. I seem to have...um, misplaced my driver."

"That is most unfortunate, sweet Guillaume. Does it make you uncomfortable?"

"A...a little."

She walked up to Guillaume and planted a kiss upon his lips. "Why have you come? Do you wish to see your sisters?"

"It is not that," said Guillaume, his voice much smoother than it had been a moment ago. "I have come to warn you of an approaching Hell Stalker. He was on his way here this morning."

"Is this the same Hell Stalker that you delivered to us a couple of days ago?"

"Yes," said Guillaume. "I thought him dead, but word reached me that he was still in Bastia. Those no-good Boutaines brothers did not do their bloody jobs properly, it seems. Worthless, the pair of them."

"It was not their fault," said the woman gently, caressing Guillaume's cheek. "We underestimated his capabilities. He escaped from right under our noses and wreaked havoc upon our beautiful little Lille. He was coming this way, you say?"

"Yes, my love."

"We have seen no sight of him nor have we heard a sound, but I shall tell my worshippers to be extra vigilant."

"I am relieved to hear that, Lady Elissar," said Guillaume. "Are they...are they..."

Lady Elissar? Caen felt a shiver run up his spine. This woman was called Elissar? Surely, she could not be the Outer World goddess; she was long dead. He could already imagine the look on Lestrange's face had he been listening in on this conversation.

"They are still as they were," said Lady Elissar, "but the ritual begins at sundown. That will be no more than an hour from now, my dear. Would you like to stay for it and you can return them home at nightfall?"

"I do not think that I should," said Guillaume, but Lady Elissar planted another kiss on him.

"Yes," he said breathlessly upon her pulling away. "I would very much like to stay, my love."

Lady Elissar pulled Guillaume inside and locked the gate behind them, leaving the concealed Caen alone outside the walls. It had taken every ounce of his restraint to not pounce and kill the pair of them on the spot, but if he revealed himself too early then the demons may have swarmed him and he could lose his chance at finding the Legot sisters alive.

What was most curious to Caen, even more so than Lady Elissar's name, was the effect that the woman had on Guillaume. Much like Leticia had doubtlessly tried to do to Caen himself, this woman was influencing Guillaume. Perhaps he had not willingly helped her kidnap his sisters after all? If his brothel visits began before the succubi had arrived in Bastia, then he was simply in the wrong place at the wrong time. For himself, at least. For the Daughters of Elissar, he was somewhere most desirable.

Caen crept out from behind the tree and pulled two apples from a pouch on his belt, tossing them to the horses who lowered their heads and started crunching. He then ran up to the wall and leapt at it, pulling himself up just enough to see over the top. He could see Lady Elissar guiding Guillaume to the ruins of the bell tower that the Iron Hound had destroyed. The demons were still surrounding the statue, but they were starting to scatter outward to keep watch around the village. Caen had to be quick.

He threw himself over the wall and hurried towards the nearest house. He forced open the window and jumped through it, finding it empty. This house smelled worse than the ones he had entered a few days prior, not least because of the rotten remains of a cat that had been pinned to the wall by a knife. After closing the window, Caen crept over to the far side of the room where another window lay.

Outside, he could see the demons wandering. He would have preferred to not get caught, but at least this time he was prepared to fight them off. The sun was sinking, but it would be almost an hour until it touched the horizon. There would be no cover of darkness if he wanted to remain stealthy and would have to rely solely on vigilance and timing.

Caen slowly opened the second window and cautiously poked his head out. There were no demons drifting in his direction, so he hopped outside and closed the window behind him before running to the broken remains of a house the Iron Hound had destroyed before his very eyes. He hurried through the gaping hole in the wooden wall and stepped over the broken glass and splintered planks of wood that littered the damaged floor.

"Krulka—" began a demon, but Caen cut its head from its body before it had the chance to finish its disgusting word.

The foul whelp slumped to the ground as its head hit the floor with a dull thud. Caen dragged the body with one hand while kicking the head along, and burying them under some rubble. It occurred to him that it may be unnecessary considering the trail of blood he had left behind that would be more than a little suspicious. Caen moved to the edge of the broken wall and kept to the shadows, awaiting any other demons that may have heard the start of their recently deceased kin's yell, but none came.

He was not far from the ruined bell tower now. If he had a clear run, he could be there within seconds and find out where Guillaume and Lady Elissar had disappeared to. He poked his head through the broken gap and looked left and right. This was his chance.

Caen dashed across the grass and leapt over the

spiked iron fence, checking over his shoulder as he did so. He dove behind a large section of tower wall that had planted itself firmly in the ground and kept low. He only heard the distant rustling of the demons and occasional low mutterings as they conversed in briefly in their foul tongue, but nothing approached him.

He crawled across the grass, making his way onto the path while trying to keep behind as much of the rubble and debris as he could. Once he was sure he was out of sight, he arose while keeping hunched over. He wandered over to the base, looking to see if anything here was amiss, but it looked exactly as a ruined tower ought to, right down to the brass bell barely visible within the centre of the stone heap.

"Where could they have gone?" Caen whispered, moving up to the least obstructed section of the tower wall and leaning over it.

There was the answer he sought, lying on the ground before him. A trapdoor. In all the chaos with the hound, Caen hadn't even considered that there would be something on the other side of the bell tower but there it was.

"I've found you, Lady Elissar," said Caen softly with a smirk. "The life feast ends without a main course, I'm afraid."

He looked around to make sure things were still quiet and then climbed over the low wall. He grabbed the trapdoor's iron handle tightly and pulled it open to reveal the darkly descending staircase it had kept secret.

With a last look glance at Lille, where the demons had mostly retreated to the walls, he walked down into the dark tunnel where the only light was from dim lanterns hung along the hidden passageway. He closed the trapdoor behind himself and took a sword in each of his hands, expecting more than just Guillaume and his mistress hiding in the shadows.

The passage was a straight line and all was quiet and still except for the intermittent flicker of the lantern's soft flames. The occasional draught entering from the world above made the hairs on the back of Caen's neck stand up. He was not expecting anything he could not defeat down here, yet he was still skittish. The past few days of trouble had all led him to this and a wrong move could spell the death of the Legot sisters.

He knew he would be paid whether the sisters were alive or not, but to know they were alive and for them to die at the last moment was unacceptable to him. Innocent life should not be snuffed out at the whim of some witch who had become an Outer World goddess millennia ago.

Caen treaded lightly, listening carefully for even a murmur that would reveal any subterranean lurkers, but there was only silence. After a short while, the path forked. The left path led to a downward staircase and the right to a small side chamber where Caen could see a statue of Elissar gazing out at him, not dissimilar to the one from the village above, but much closer in size to Caen himself.

He wandered into the empty room and looked upon the statue. If this was a true depiction of the goddess, she was indeed beautiful. He could see how men would fall for her and a hint of persuasion would make them endlessly devoted. Once magic was thrown into the mix, she could have had the entirety of the Outer World at her beck and call.

The statue bore a bronze plaque at the base and Caen could only just make out the words in the low light.

> O our mother, so tender and fair
> We beg your ear to hear our prayer
> With beauty unbound and endless grace
> What we would do to restore your face
> Such beauty, such youth, never to age
> We curse the one who placed the cage
> Upon your soul, and stole your life
> Leaving your daughters in unending strife
> We will become you, the time is now
> Your name will live through us, this we vow

"Utter madness," Caen whispered to himself upon finishing the twisted prayer.

He knew now that the woman that he had seen with Guillaume was not the true Elissar, simply an imposter who had stolen her name and perhaps even her face. Did this *Lady Elissar* hope to become a goddess herself?

A far cry from an easy task and Caen was certain that Lestrange would scoff at such a notion. Whatever this woman was planning, there could be no doubt that if the Legot sisters were the first victims—which seemed increasingly unlikely—they would most certainly not be the last.

Chapter 11

Stolen Beauty

Caen crept down the staircase of the cold and damp passage, his determination to find the missing Legot sisters greater than ever. Lady Elissar would meet her end today and Guillaume would have to answer for everything he had done, whether he was spellbound or not.

The Hell Stalker reached the bottom of the staircase and paused upon hearing the faint echo of a voice drifting up the corridor. There was someone coming, but there was nowhere to hide. Caen hurriedly snuffed out two of the lanterns and drew his crossbow right before a robed silhouette of a woman appeared from around the corner.

He waited quietly, knowing the woman would see him before long. He wasn't quite sure what his plan was and would have to improvise. She suddenly stopped, having seen the intruder, and Caen shot a bolt through her shin as she turned to run. She let out a scream and he darted towards her, drawing one of his swords and holding it to her neck as he pulled her to her feet.

"Eloise," called another woman's voice from somewhere in the tunnels. "Are you alright?"

"The lantern is out, you fell down the stairs," Caen whispered to her as he held her to the blade. "Do not call her by her name." He did not trust the young woman to alert the other woman by giving a false name.

"The...the lantern is out," called Eloise, her eyes fearful but her voice remarkably composed. "I tripped on the stairs. I cut my knee, that is all. I will be back shortly."

"A little too much detail for my liking," said Caen quietly.

"I did not alert her to anything, I swear it!" whimpered Eloise.

Caen dragged her back down the corridor and up the stairs, wary that another of the Daughters of Elissar may suspect foul play. Once they were back in the room with the statue, he breathed a little easier.

"You, girl," he said while drawing his second blade. "Are you a demon or a human?"

"Human," she said, her voice still composed.

"Demon, then," he said, "but I know you can still feel fear. The Legot sisters, where are they?"

"I would die before I tell you," said Eloise.

Caen smiled before shoving her back and hacking off one of her hands in a single swift strike. Eloise held back a scream of pain as she released her illusory form and revealed herself as a succubus—exactly as Caen had suspected.

"Such...such cruelty," she cried, careful to keep her voice low in fear of Caen's retaliation. "My beautiful...my beautiful hand."

Caen pulled out his second sword and twirled it around. "I have killed your kind before and I have crippled you. You know I have no qualms about ending your life, yet you would rather die than reveal to me what it is I want to know? Would you rather I mutilate you further, hellspawn? Do not tempt me."

Eloise's pointed tail swayed as she clutched her bleeding wound. "They're down below," she said. "I've told you what you wanted to know, now let me go."

"You thought it would be that simple?" chuckled Caen. "Answer a single question and you have your freedom? Perhaps I'd even give you a sack of apples and a jar of honey to enjoy after dinner? No, my dear Elosie, your knowledge of this place is greater than mine and I can use that."

"Please," begged Eloise, dropping to her knees as her tail and horns vanished, masking her as human once again. "I did not choose this life. I was dragged into it, turned into what I am today by the cruel Lady Elissar. She's...she's the real monster. You must believe me!"

Eloise began to weep and she crawled forward to Caen, grabbing onto his leg. He kicked her aside and pushed the tip of his blade into her stomach. The succubus's beautiful face turned into a horrific grimace as she cursed with rage.

"I can feel you already trying to work your magic on me, but it's of no use," said Caen sternly.

"You think I would let you kiss me and bring me under your enchantment? This will be your last warning before I lose my temper, succubus. And I suggest that you do not disrobe, for I can still kill you easily with my eyes fixed elsewhere."

"You're no paladin or priest," growled Eloise, standing up as her grimace vanished. "You must be the Hell Stalker. I will tell you what you want to know if you permit me to live once our business is concluded."

"Agreed," said Caen, glad to see that this demon valued her life, disgracefully led as it may have been. "Who is Lady Elissar? Is she your leader?"

"Yes. One of very few humans among us. As you well know, Hell Stalker, no human who has become a demon with an impure soul can ascend to godhood. It is impossible. Therefore, to take up the mantle of Elissar, our matriarch must remain entirely herself until that day comes."

Caen had guessed correctly, but it did not make him feel better. "And this life feast is part of that process?" he asked.

Eloise smiled menacingly. "Yes."

Caen shoved one blade straight through her gut and whipped the other sword around, cutting the head from the lunging succubus that had miserably failed to sneak up behind him. The two succubi dropped dead before the statue of their goddess with their blood slowly filling the gaps between the stones on the floor.

"Such a shame, I thought I had found a trustworthy demon," Caen said sarcastically to Eloise's body. "My search will continue, perhaps forevermore."

He knew that time was running out and the

ritual would begin at any moment so he had better hurry. He didn't have the opportunity to ask how many more of the Daughters awaited him. Caen would take no pleasure in having to kill the human women, but they had chosen their unfortunate fates, not him.

He hurried back to where he had first encountered Eloise and pressed ahead. He could hear murmurings deeper in and followed them through the tight tunnels until he saw a lengthy broken section of wall that overlooked a large, misty cavern. He kept low and close to the wall which looked to have collapsed recently, so freshly rough was the stone.

Atop a set of stairs was a large platform with a grand stone wall covered in runic inscriptions. In the centre of the wall was an emerging statue of Elissar, who held up her unmoving hands as though to invite those in her presence to ascend. Illuminated by two large stone braziers were a dozen Daughters of Elissar—all human or pretending to be—with their leader, Lady Elissar, standing at the centre.

She had pulled her hood back, revealing a shining wave of black hair and the most perfectly crafted face that Caen had ever laid eyes on. She was immaculately beautiful, evident even from a distance, with a delicate nose, high cheekbones and dazzling eyes that could ensnare even the most faithful of men. The Hell Stalker had to remind himself that she was a wicked woman who conspired with demons and that this was not her true face.

Guillaume Legot was looking toward the leader of the Daughters of Elissar while kneeling at the top of the stairs. He looked completely mesmerised and his face was unburdened, as though he was in a trance.

With a wave of Lady Elissar's hand, he shimmied aside while remaining on his knees as four demon whelps—the same kind as those from the village outside—carried a wooden cage containing two thin figures up the stairs and placed it at the statue's feet. It was them; Amélie and Celine Legot. They were indeed alive, but they were dishevelled and looked utterly terrified.

"The time draws near, my sisters," said Lady Elissar in a commanding yet silky voice that echoed throughout the cavern. "This month's feast is upon us and the two fairest girls in Bastia are ours for the taking. Gaze upon their faces."

Caen pulled out his crossbow and aimed it carefully at Lady Elissar as her demonic minions scurried back down the stairs. She had started walking around the circle and he wanted a clear shot to end this as quickly as possible.

"My sisters, we will dine well on youth and beauty this evening. Our esteemed guest, Guillaume, has kindly offered to return these innocent girls home so they can enjoy their remaining few days in quiet peace. Isn't that so kind of him?"

The sisters all murmured in agreement as Guillaume continued to stare, enthralled.

"A dutiful brother who loves his sisters so dearly. Isn't that right, my dear?"

"Yes, my love," said Guillaume breathlessly while his sisters watched on with tears streaming down their freckled cheeks. "I love them so, but I love you more."

"And now," said Lady Elissar, returning to the centre of the circle and untying her robe, "we begin."

Her robes fell to the floor as did the robes of the rest of the sisters and they all stood naked in their circle. Had Caen been a weak man, he would have buckled, for the women all had hourglass bodies with plump, round breasts and perfectly flat stomachs. Most perfect of all was Lady Elissar whose hips could have borne a brood of a dozen children who could conquer the world yet her body would remain immaculate.

The Daughters of Elissar joined hands as Lady Elissar turned to face the statue. Caen held his breath and pressed upon the trigger of his crossbow. The bolt tore across the cavern, but Caen's eyes widened in horror as it bounced off of nothing and was cast aside, having come within feet of the perfect woman.

The women all turned to face Caen, most of them with twisted faces as their illusions slipped. Lady Elissar held up a hand without averting her gaze from the statue and began to chant. The palms of the Elissar statue began to glow and Caen suddenly realised his folly. Lady Elissar had known he was coming, of course, and that a simple spell was all that was needed to deflect an attempted assassination. His crossbow was useless to him up here and he could not jump into the cavern without breaking his ankles.

Horrified, he stood up and ran down the passageway, looking for another way down. He slung his crossbow back over his shoulder and drew his twin blades, praying under his breath that he wasn't too late. The wall had indeed been broken recently, perhaps even within the last ten minutes, and it was no doubt to bait him into wasting his time while the ritual proceeded uninterrupted.

He leapt down a set of stairs and came face to face with the four demon whelps who had carried the Legot sisters. They did not even have time to react as he swung each sword deftly, cutting through their foul bodies with nary a care given. Caen was gone before the blood-spouting demons even hit the tunnel floor.

He rounded the corner which opened into a large room, but it was not the cavern he sought. Caen's heart sank as he saw the beast that stood before him. Its skin was stretched and the bloody gaps glowed orange while its black metal plates shielded its vital organs. Upon laying eyes on the Hell Stalker, it growled as viscous saliva dripped from its mouth, forming a puddle on the floor.

Caen clenched his swords, not taking his eyes off the Iron Hound, which crouched down, ready to pounce. All the while, the ritual continued somewhere ahead. He had better make this kill a quick one or everything he had worked for was for nothing.

The furious beast leapt at Caen who swiftly dove forward and rolled underneath it, swinging his swords upwards as he rose to his feet. To his dismay, the blades clanged against the unseen plating underneath the demonic canine who spun around and swiped at Caen, tearing his cloak while narrowly missing the Hell Stalker's shoulder.

It lunged forward with its open mouth and Caen threw himself against the wall. Upon his foe taking another step forward, he slinked aside and the beast bashed its head into the stone and cracked dozens of bricks, which trickled dust to the floor as the hound moved aside and swiped at his intended next meal.

As much as Lestrange had claimed the beast was a dumb brute, Caen could see the look on its face. It was truly vengeful and had saved space in the pit of its stomach for this one specific human who had humiliated it so.

Caen stepped back, blocking and parrying the swinging claws of the infernal dog with solid steel but, with each strike, his grip weakened. The powerful beast was strong and well-armoured. Even with his weapons, he could not take it on so easily. He had to be clever. It was just a big dog in armour, after all, and he knew where dogs could not easily reach. The only problem was baiting it effectively without losing an arm.

"Come on, you filthy mongrel," spat Caen, slashing his sword out in a whipping arc as the hound swiftly leapt back.

The Hell Stalker raised his two swords overhead, bringing them down at the beast's dripping nose, only to be intercepted by a single claw that brushed aside both weapons with its blackened nails. Caen threw his arms out exaggeratedly and the beast took the bait.

As the hound lunged for him with its sharp-toothed mouth ready to devour the human whole, he jumped atop its head and ran onto its back. He shoved his twin blades in a gap between the armoured plates, causing the hound to howl in pain. Caen clung to his swords as the beast spun around, trying to shake him off, but the metal only sank deeper and deeper until it ground against the canine's bones.

It tried to swing at him, but its legs could not bend around to reach him. It tried whipping at the Hell Stalker with its tail, but it was not strong enough to do much more than annoy him, for it was not like the whipping tail of a succubus. As it swung once more, Caen pulled a single sword free and flung his arm back, slicing the tip of the Iron Hound's tail clean off.

The beast cried out a fearful howl that echoed throughout the chamber and then fell onto its side. Caen twisted the blade still wedged in the hound's back before jumping to safety, causing further agony to his foe. The Iron Hound winced and twitched as it forced itself back onto its feet.

Seizing the opportunity brought by his enemy's momentary collapse, Caen clutched his remaining sword in both hands and thrust it deep into one of the creature's orange eyes, piercing it with a sickening pop. Blood burst out as the Hell Stalker pushed with all his might and skewered the Iron Hound through its brain. So tough was the beast that it still tried to take a final swing at him, but its strength waned and it fell back onto the ground; it was dead at last.

Caen pulled his other sword free from its back and ran to the far side of the room and into a smaller passageway which soon opened up into the cavern he sought. The hands of the Elissar statue continued to glow a faint blue as a flurry of small orbs of light were pulled from the cage holding the Legot sisters. The orbs flowed around the circle before being drawn into the naked Lady Elissar.

There could not be much time left and Caen bounded up the staircase, only for Guillaume to step in front of him to block the way. Lord Legot's son gave the Hell Stalker a furious look as he held out his sword with a trembling arm. "You shall not disturb, my love," he said with feigned confidence before lunging at Caen.

The Hell Stalker stepped aside and pulled Guillaume's outstretched arm, throwing the nobleman off balance and teetering on the edge of a step. Caen turned and kicked Guillaume in the back, sending the foolish young man flying to the bottom of the staircase where he hit his head on the stone while letting out a pained groan.

Caen didn't afford the disgraced lord's son a second glance as he thrust his sword into the back of the nearest of the Daughters, who screamed as she fell to her knees with blood streaming from her open would. Her falling body broke the circle and the ritual ended with the glow fading from the statue and the last of the orbs of light disappearing into wispy nothingness.

Lady Elissar turned to look at Caen with a delicate smile upon her face. It almost seemed impossible, but she was more beautiful than ever before. Caen shut his eyes tightly for a moment to remember why he was there before reopening them. She was absolutely radiant and he knew that without the power of his brand warding off the worst of her enchantment, he would be on his knees before her.

"You are too late, you pathetic Hell Stalker," said Lady Elissar, her enticing voice pulling him in even with the insult she uttered.

She and the rest of the Daughters of Elissar lifted their robes from the ground and covered their naked bodies. Lady Elissar held out her arm and gestured towards the cage where two old and withered women lay moaning feebly as they clung to the bars. Caen stood in shock as he watched the unrecognisable Legot sisters.

"What...what have you done?" Caen muttered, horrified at the sight of the aged girls. Their beauty and youth had been stolen from them; ripped away and leaving the young girls as withered husks.

"They have served a greater purpose," said Lady Elissar, placing her hands upon her heart and letting out a long exhalation. "You are free to return them to their father, Hell Stalker. I am sure he will reward you all the same. You can tell him whatever falsehood you please. You can even tell him that I am dead if that will get you your money. I assure you that Guillaume will back your story if I ask him to. And I will, *if* you leave here at once and promise never to return."

Such arrogance to think that Caen would simply walk away, yet his swords fell from his hands and he dropped to his knees before the witch.

"I...I cannot simply leave," he said to her breathlessly while staring into her sapphire-like eyes. "It would be too much for me to turn my back on you, Lady Elissar. I cannot bear to be without you, my love."

Chapter 12

A Grim Fate

The Daughters of Elissar stared at Caen with a look of deep satisfaction upon their beautiful faces. The most satisfied and the most beautiful of all was Lady Elissar, her radiance enhanced by the youth of the Legot sisters who lay weak as old women in their cage.

"You cannot be without me?" asked Lady Elissar, walking toward Caen and placing her hand upon his cheek.

The touch of her palm upon his face was ambrosia and Caen now truly understood why a man as weak and pathetic as Guillaume was so susceptible to the will of the lady. The sight of her was something to behold, but her touch? It was everything.

"No, my love," he said to her, his voice much lighter than usual. "I must stay with you for eternity. I will be your guardian, defending you from those who would dare to do you harm. I pledge myself to you, for you are my world."

Lestrange's words ran through his head. Elissar herself was not simply a goddess of beauty; she was a goddess of vanity. With vanity, came arrogance. Arrogance that she demonstrated so readily in thinking that she could convince a Hell Stalker to leave her be. Caen did not know what magic this witch possessed, and he did not know how to counter that which he knew nothing of, but he thought perhaps he did not need to.

"You see, my beloved sisters," said Lady Elissar, turning to the other Daughters. "We have grown so strong and so beautiful that even a Hell Stalker's innate protection against enchantments is not enough to resist our beauty. In time, all will come to love us the same way and devote themselves without reservation."

"Glory to us," the Daughters said in unison.

"Let me take Guillaume Legot's place," said Caen desperately, placing his hands on the ground and bowing to kiss Lady Elissar's feet. "He is weak and I am strong. He does not deserve your attention and I can bring you whoever you desire for the next life feast. I beg of you, my queen of eternal grace."

"Arise, Hell Stalker," said Lady Elissar, "and tell me your name."

"My name is Caen, my love," he said, staring into her eyes and doing everything he could to fight against the alluring magic that was trying to penetrate his defences.

Lady Elissar placed both of her palms upon Caen's cheeks and pulled him into a kiss. This was his chance, she was in the depths of her influence and arrogance, but Caen felt weak as the beautiful enchantress kissed him. His arms grew limp from reservation as he felt his burdens be lifted by Lady Elissar's magic, but he had to act now. If he did not, he would be broken and fall under her spell entirely. He could not let himself die for her.

"Ah," gasped Lady Elissar, as her eyes shot wide open in terror. She stepped back, trembling as Caen drew his knife back. She glanced at her stomach, where there was a gaping wound from which blood poured across the floor. "Wh-wh...why?"

The Hell Stalker thrust his knife straight into her chest, piercing her heart as the other Daughters charged towards Caen. He flung his knife into one of their throats and sidestepped the grasp of the succubus as he retrieved his swords from the ground.

The Daughters of Elissar attacked him relentlessly, but these were not demons designed for combat. No, they were weak. Caen cut each and every one of them down, even the human Daughters who were foolish enough to not plead for their lives—not that he would have spared them. It was not long before the entire coven was strewn across the ground, never again to perform the life.

Caen looked toward the cage and his heart grew heavy with all of his burdens returned to him. The Legot sisters were still there and they were still old and decrepit. He rushed over to twins and tugged on the iron lock that sealed them within the cage, but it was sturdy. The cage, however, was not as strong. Caen thrust his elbow down upon the wooden bars and snapped them, pulling the cage apart and lifting the Legot sisters out one by one. They were in tears and looked to each other before staring at their frail hands.

"We are...we are still old," croaked one of them despairingly. "Even with the death of the witch, we're...this."

"Which one are you?" Caen asked her.

"Amélie."

"Amélie," said Caen, placing his hands upon her bony shoulders. "I will deliver you both to a man who may be able to cure you of this affliction, but we must escape from here. There are still demons above who may turn feral with their mistress dead. Make no mistake that we are still in grave danger in Lille."

Amélie nodded, her eyes filling with tears once again, and Celine looked toward the staircase with fear. Caen spun around and saw Guillaume weakly walking towards them, rubbing his head with his left hand. He held up his right hand to show that he was not armed.

"Please," he said as he drew close. "Please, Caen, I wish you no harm."

Caen sheathed his swords as the young man walked up beside him. Guillaume sighed in relief before Caen's solid fist collided with his cheek, toppling him. He lay on the ground, cowering as Caen stood above him.

"My actions were not my own!" he cried out, terrified. "I swear to you!"

"That will be for your father to judge," said Caen, grabbing Guillaume by his shirt and pulling him to his feet. "Do you wish to atone for what you have seen done to your sisters?"

"Yes," said Guillaume, nodding vigorously before turning to the twins. "My precious sisters...I am so sorry. I promise you that I will use whatever money and influence I have to return you to your former selves. You do not deserve to have a brother as pathetic as I..."

"Apologies can wait, Guillaume," said Caen.

"Just tell me what I must do. I will do whatever it takes."

"Are you a good runner?"

"I...I suppose th—"

"Yes or no?"

"Yes."

"Good," said Caen, slapping Guillaume on the shoulder. "You can carry Celine and I will carry Amélie. I doubt I can take on all of the demons above at the same time and I would be surprised if you could take a single one even with a divine blade given by the True One himself, so we're going to make a break for the wall and get back to your carriage."

"But my driver has disappeared," said Guillaume solemnly.

"Yes, that was my doing. You're so witless that you did not realise that I brought you all the from Bastia. Luckily for you, I am not such a simpleton. If you do as I say, I will ensure that all of us stay alive."

Guillaume looked overwhelmed as his eyes returned to his aged sisters, but he nodded and approached a terrified Celine.

"No," she said, backing away. "I will not go anywhere with you...look what you did!"

She started hitting her brother, but she was so feeble that it barely wrinkled his shirt. Caen approached her and took her hands gently.

"Please, Celine," he said. "He has wronged you beyond comprehension, but if we are to return you to your true age, we need his help. As strong as I am, I suspect I would be swiftly overpowered by the demons waiting above. I do not fight well in large crowds, my dear...will you let him carry you?"

Celine looked at her brother coldly, but she nodded. "I will."

"I did not...I should not have..." muttered Guillaume, only to be ignored.

Caen hoisted Amélie onto his back and then Guillaume hoisted Celine onto his. The two departed from the chamber while holding the twins tightly and marched back through the passageways. Caen could tell that the pampered Guillaume was tiring already, light as Celine was, but he did not complain. The Hell Stalker truly hoped that Lord Legot's son was a completely unwilling participant in the horror of the recent life feast.

Upon reaching the trapdoor, Caen and Guillaume set the girls-turned-old women down. Caen opened the door carefully and saw the dark blue of the night sky above them. There was no rain or wind to speak of to mask their escape, so he himself would have to serve as the distraction to give Guillaume and Celine their chance.

He stepped outside and kept low. Thankfully, the demons were scattered enough and still patrolling the village. They must still have been following their last orders from Lady Elissar, completely unaware of her death. This would only aid the chance of a successful escape.

Caen returned to the trapdoor and opened it, holding up a hand to stop Guillaume from coming up. "I will take Amélie with me on my back and make for the far wall at the opposite side of the gate," he said. "I will try to remain as unseen as I can. When I call out to draw the demons to me, you are to take Celine and return to the wagon. Get yourselves safely inside and keep the door open until I return. Do you understand?"

"Yes," said Guillaume with anxiety plastered across his face.

"Good," said Caen, taking Amélie in his arms. "Remember, don't run until you hear my call."

Caen scrambled past the rubble and leapt over the iron fence as demons slowly started taking notice of him. It was a short way to the wall, but he took a longer path and weaved between the spaced-out houses to draw in more demons. There was already a dozen of them following him, but he wanted to make it at least two dozen to give Guillaume and Celine the clearest path possible.

"Are you alright?" he asked Amélie who clung to him.

"Yes," she lied.

Caen respected that in spite of her youth and the immense trauma she had lived through this week, she still had the fortitude to soldier on. He was determined to see her back home, money or no money.

He continued to run, drawing in more demons who picked up their own pace to chase after him. He finally let himself reach the wall and turned to face his foes. He did not have time to count, but he trusted that he had attracted enough attention. He drew a deep breath and yelled so loudly that the birds in the woods scattered into the night sky.

Caen charged forward with Amélie holding as tightly as she could to him. He moved through the demons, avoiding their lunges and swipes as best as he could. He was forced to barge a few of them out of the way, but he made it through with only a few fresh cuts to the face and neck for his troubles.

He passed by the ruins of the bell tower that had masked the fallen village's terrible secret and could see the shadow of Guillaume by the gate. There were demons moving towards him, but he was already raising Celine up shakily to get her to safety. She fell over the gate and onto the path and the young nobleman clambered after her as a demon reached for his leg. He was down a shoe, but he had made it outside.

As Caen ran, the two Legot siblings disappeared into the wagon and the door was left open as a half dozen demons wrenched the gate open.

"Over here," called Caen, sprinting towards them.

The hellspawn turned to him, their mangled faces looking at him with hunger, but he would not satiate their appetite. He would not grant them the feast they so desired. He rammed through them, knocking half of the pack to the ground and leaving the others stumbling forward as they reached for him.

He charged through the open gate and threw Amélie to her brother, who caught her and then sealed the door tightly. Caen hopped atop the driver's seat and cried out to the horses, startling them enough that they immediately started running. He steered them away as the demons gave chase, but they would not gain on the carriage. Caen would not let them.

*

"There is nothing that can be done?" Lord Legot asked Lestrange, who pushed his spectacles back up his face.

Caen had brought the scholar to the manor, assuring the lord that if anyone could aid his daughters it was Lestrange. The Hell Stalker was staring out the window as the sun rose above the horizon. He was admiring the beautiful garden and wondering if his life would ever be boring enough for him to have a garden of his own. Would he even want that?

"I did not say that nothing can be done," said Lestrange, "what I said was that I cannot undo the magic. It may have been easier if Lady Elissar was still alive to retrieve your daughters' stolen youth from, but...well, I will say nothing further on that."

"I did what I could," said Caen softly. "If I hadn't killed her when I did, she would have broken me."

"Yes," sighed Lord Legot, the pain behind his eyes evident. "I am grateful of course that you returned them to me, but...you must know the sorrow that this horrible situation causes a father. To see his daughters older than he? With months, if not weeks to live? Am I to make them comfortable and then say goodbye or spend their remaining time trying to restore their youth to them? I do not know...I...I simply do not know."

"My best advice," said Lestrange, "is to bring

them to the temple and leave them with the priests. Their divine magic may be able to prolong their lives while I research a way to reverse what has been done to them."

"And you will start at once?" asked Lord Legot.

"I will need funds to hasten the process," said Lestrange. "The books and reagents will not come cheaply. Sadly, they never do."

"I will pay whatever you need," said Lord Legot defiantly. "I will give up my entire fortune if need be. I will live as a pauper until my dying day. That rat, Guillaume, will see none of it."

Even with Caen giving his thoughts on Guillaume's state of mind when he abducted his own sisters, Lord Legot refused to believe that he had not acted of his own free will. So stung was he by the betrayal of his own son that he had summoned the guards in the dead of night and had Guillaume thrown in the cells.

"I will begin immediately," said Lestrange, bowing his head. "I wish you well, Lord Legot."

"Thank you," said the lord, his voice raspy. "Thank you, both of you."

"Farewell, Lord Legot," said Caen, giving the distraught father a sympathetic nod.

Caen and Lestrange departed from the manor, not saying a word to each other until they were past the garden gates.

"Do you think it's possible to return them to their true ages?" asked Caen as he and Lestrange wandered down the quiet street.

"Are you accusing me of trying to siphon coin from an easy source?" asked Lestrange, pretending to be affronted.

"No," said Caen, "but the thought had crossed

my mind."

Lestrange chuckled briefly before returning to his usual dry tone. "I believe it's possible, but I don't think the ritual can be reversed with Lady Elissar dead. I think life will need to be siphoned from others in some fashion, but I am not sure how simple that will be. Whatever the case, I must work quickly."

"A shame I won't be around to see it," said Caen, looking to the sky.

"You're leaving town?"

"My friend," said the Hell Stalker, "I am wealthier than I have ever been and I wish to enjoy it for a short while. I cannot do that here."

"Why not?"

"Because the Boutaines brothers will come looking for their share."

"And you are unwilling to pay them what you promised them?"

"Pay them?" scoffed Caen. "I've repaid you what I owe you, plus a little extra for your troubles—"

"And it is appreciated," said Lestrange.

"Indeed," replied Caen. "But the Boutaines brothers deserve nothing. Lord Legot knows that they interfered on Guillaume's request. I'm sure he'll pull a few strings and see them driven from Bastia. No doubt, they'll come looking for me, but I'll be well away from here by that time."

"You always say this place bores you, then you come back a few months later," said Lestrange. "I suspect you'll do the same again, the Boutaines be damned."

"Each time I come into town, my good deeds are forgotten."

"I suspect that will not be the case this time,"

said Lestrange, uncharacteristically upbeat. "I'm sure word will reach the other Hell Stalkers of what happened here and your standing within the organisation will see a nice little jump."

"Perhaps it will, my friend," said Caen daring to hope, "perhaps it will."

"Do you have a destination in mind?" asked Lestrange, as the two wandered into the town square where traders were setting up their stalls.

"I think I'll take a short trip to Autun before moving along," said Caen. "A new friend of mine could probably use a hand, presuming he's still there."

"Is this the fellow who helped you after your first run-in with the Iron Hound?"

"It is, but his name escapes me."

"Henri."

"Yes, that was it. I had better write it down."

Caen and Lestrange walked past the fountain nestled in the centre of Bastia's town square. The water from the stone lion's mouth hit the pool beneath and sprayed little droplets at Caen, who stopped and turned towards it.

He reached into a pouch on his belt and pulled out a small silver coin. He wished that the Legot sisters would see their youth restored to them and would go on to live full and happy lives. With a smile, he flicked the coin into the fountain and returned to walking as the silver piece sank to the bottom of the water.

Epilogue

What a horrid day to have one of your unrealised fears come to pass. Caen could see the faint shadows on the curtain passing by as he lay paralysed in the shack. He glanced towards the door and was minorly relieved to see that it was barricaded; at least the prince had done him the decency of slowing the demons down, but it would not be long before they were gnawing on his flesh and he could not do a thing about it.

He had been poisoned by a Blood Moon assassin while pursuing a kidnapped lord across the Empire of Warth. Along the way, he encountered Prince Gresten Lochmeria and Edith of Warth while they slept in an abandoned tower. He had enlisted them to help him out so that he wasn't mauled in a town of demons where he sought information, but he knew now that he should have left them to their own devices.

How was he to know that Edith was a target of the Blood Moons? Of course, he had tried to do the noble thing and throw her out of the way of the assassin's poisoned knife only to be pierced by it himself. Why bother trying to do the right thing if this was where it would lead?

There was a scraping sound coming from the door. "Fantastic," Caen mumbled to himself as he listened to a demon's sharp nails trying to claw their way through the wood.

He suddenly realised that he had spoken. Every other attempt to speak since being stricken with this paralysis was incomprehensible babble followed by an embarrassing dribbling. Could this mean that the poison was finally starting to wear off? Did he owe it to the passing of time or was it the power of his brand? He flicked his tongue around his mouth. There was still a hint of tingling in it, but he could control it.

Caen tried to move one of his arms and found that it shifted ever so slightly. He attempted to clench his fist and his fingers contracted weakly, but they did indeed move. How much longer until he regained full control of his body? He wondered this while also wondering how much longer it would be until he was not the only one in this ramshackle little house.

"Weapons," he uttered, looking around but unable to see himself. "What weapons do I have?"

He forced his neck to turn, pointing his head towards the ceiling and then lowered his eyes. Past his sharp nose and pointed chin, he could see one sword strapped to his waist while the other was no doubt trodden into the muddy ground outside in this filthy little village in the wetlands. No matter, for a single sword would be more than enough if he could just manage to grip it.

Caen wriggled his fingers trying to bring some feeling back to them. He moved his left shoulder up and down and bent his arm at the elbow. He didn't even care if the rest of his body remained limp, he just needed one arm to defend himself with for the time being.

The scraping stopped and suddenly turned into a banging as the demon bashed on the door. There was the distinct crack of splintering wood that followed and Caen knew it would be only moments before the demon got fed up with the wood resisting it and smashed the door to pieces. It would not be much longer than that before it moved the makeshift barricade of furniture aside and came for him.

"This is not my end," Caen muttered, "this is not my end."

He grasped the handle of his sword and held it with all his might. He dragged his arm upwards, haphazardly unsheathing the sharp blade. He could not muster the energy to hold the glistening weapon high, but he was relieved to have it in his hand. There was a comfort to holding a sword, no matter the situation.

"Lestrange was right," he said, the corner of his mouth twitching into an irked smile, "I should have learned magic and saved myself a lot of hassle."

One of the door planks snapped, leaving a hole in the entranceway, and through the gap appeared the face of a demon whelp. It wore the clothes of the former villagers, but it was not fooling anyone, certainly not with those stubby horns protruding from its dome. It smiled menacingly as it pushed itself through the door and then shoved the furniture out of the way.

"Do not beg, do not plead," said Caen to himself as the demon rushed towards him. "If this is indeed the end, then go out with your soul intact. True One, please bless me."

A shove and a squelch as the demon's head was run through by the sword. Caen dropped his blade, his grip failing him. More would come soon, he knew that, but he had survived the first attacker and could breathe for a moment.

He reached down and grabbed at the cloth just above his knee and pulled his leg to the side. It slid off the bed and onto the floor, his boot hitting the rotting wood with a loud thump. He had felt the impact; sensation was returning to his lower body. He grabbed the other leg and threw it to the floor too. Another thump and more feeling. He grunted as he forced himself to stand, only to keel over and fall on top of the dead demon that was sprawled across the blood-soaked planks.

As Caen reached for the bed to pull himself up, a second demon ran into the room with a look of hunger stretched across its face. It dived on top of him, intent on making him its next meal. Caen grabbed at its throat, holding it back from biting him, but it swiped at his arms, tearing apart his jacket and his leather armour with ease and making deep cuts into his skin.

With a cry of pain, the Hell Stalker mustered all of his strength and threw it back. He reached over to the sword still embedded in the first demon and wrenched it free. As the second demon pounced once more, he skewered it through its wretched gut and kicked it aside while its entrails spilt out.

Caen pulled himself back onto the bed, the sword now firmly in his hand once more. "Almost there," he said, rapping a fist on his legs which had now regained most of their sensation. He took a deep breath and arose, stumbling towards the wall and propping himself up. There were many more left outside, so it was only a matter of time, but he was ready now. He would not die this day.

The Hollow Realms
by Jordan Allen

Hollow Kingdom (2023)

A sword and sorcery tale of a prince trying to reclaim his kingdom and solve the mystery of his father and brother's fates.

Ashes of the Necropolis (2023)

A mercenary seeks his missing companions in a city filled with the undead and at the mercy of a wicked lich.

Moonlit Soul (2023)

The tale of an assassin and the paladin he's targeting on their separate journeys destined to converge.

Hollow Empire (2024)

Prince Gresten ventures to the Empire of Warth and is coerced to do the bidding of the nation's gods who seek a powerful artifact of a lost god.

Other Works by Jordan Allen

Mutagenesis: The New World (2021)

A post-apocalyptic sci-fi novel set in Texas decades after hordes of mutants wiped out civilisation. It's a tale of survival, adventure and coming to terms with misfortune.

Mutagenesis: Human Regression (2024)

Jason Cooper ventures across the wild wasteland of Texas in search of his missing sisters, finding himself up against mutants, cultists and cyborgs.